WELCOME TO HELL

Curiosity about the town's name caused ex-lawdog Carl Simpson to make a detour towards Hell. He was to regret his action when Taw McAdam took Carl's horse and abandoned him in the desert. To make matters worse, Abel Cross and his boys came by and refused to give Simpson a stirrup. Before he knew it, Carl was in a range war, on the wrong end of a bushwhacker's gun. But his troubles didn't end there and it soon became clear to Carl that only guts and blazing guns would see him through the violent times ahead.

WELCOME TO HELL

by
Elliot Long

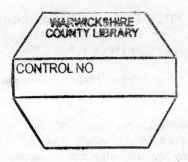

Dales Large Print Books
Long Preston, North Yorkshire,
England.

British Library Cataloguing in Publication Data.

Long, Elliot
  Welcome to Hell.

  A catalogue record for this book is
  available from the British Library

  ISBN 1-85389-912-7 pbk

First published in Great Britain by Robert Hale Ltd., 1998

Cover illustration © Prieto by arrangement with Norma Editorial S.A.

The right of Elliot Long to be identified as the author of this work has been asserted by him in accordance with the Copyright, Designs and Patents Act, 1988

Published in Large Print 1999 by arrangement with Robert Hale Ltd.

Dales Large Print is an imprint of
Library Magna Books Ltd.
Printed and bound in Great Britain by
T.J. International Ltd., Cornwall, PL28 8RW.

ONE

Carl Simpson's keen gaze missed nothing of the lonely, barren country he was passing through. But, God, it seemed to go on for ever. And the heat just ate into a man, was without mercy. Paused now on the top of this rocky mesa he shook his head. Once more, like so many times in the past, he briefly wondered what the hell he was doing here. After what had happened at Ladderet, he wished he didn't have this urge driving him all the time—that of always wanting to know what was over the next hill, so he could maybe bury the past there.

But never one to wallow in self-pity, he clicked at the roan he was riding and threaded it down the stepped, rugged slopes atop of which he'd paused. Again on the floor of this semi-desert he headed south, bound for the town of Hell. He'd already figured the name was interesting enough to make the diversion worth while; that it merited at least a peek at it before he headed into the blue Pecon Hills yonder, then on to California.

Maybe half an hour passed before he began to see what looked to be carrion gathering ahead. They came gliding in from all points of the compass, riding the hot currents of air. They began to land at a place a mile or so ahead of him.

Because of the distance they appeared as black, charred-paper shapes first off but as he got closer he confirmed what he had already guessed—that they were buzzards. That caused his lips to tighten, his gut to chill. In this merciless land, that could only mean one thing. Someone, or something, was dead out there, or getting close to it.

When he reached the site he found it was a horse that was causing all the interest. Its eyes had already been pecked out and a lone coyote was tearing at its guts until it became aware of him and loped off a short distance, only to then sit and gaze at him balefully, waiting for him to go.

Simpson stared at the horse. It clearly had a broken leg. The lower part of the hind cannon dangled loose, the bone showing yellow-white. It had been shot dead centre, in the diamond just above the eyes. Somebody had managed to extricate the saddle. Simpson could see the sweat-shape of it still etched on the horse's back. He narrowed his grey gaze. Well, whoever it was carrying that hunk of leather wouldn't get far in this grinding heat, of that he was sure.

Following the ill-defined boot tracks as they moved away from the scene he headed out. He soon found the abandoned saddle, then an empty canteen a mile on from there, then an old Spencer carbine. He took time to pick them all up as he moved along, but thought he could be wasting his time.

A mile on he eased the roan to a stop and stared ahead. He had the feeling he should be seeing something by now—some body sprawled out dying or dead on this sepia, stony ground. He considered it odd that he hadn't done.

He clicked for the roan to move on, feeling the skin on his back commencing to crawl, the hairs on the nape of his neck beginning to rise. He was starting to get a bad feeling about this. The man ahead must be a tenderfoot, or had been driven into the desert before he could take the proper precautions. And that would make him a possible owlhoot.

As Simpson topped the long rise he had been negotiating he stared out across the yucca- and saguaro-studded flatlands before him. Yeah, maybe a quarter of a mile ahead. There he was, sprawled face down on the ground.

Simpson approached cautiously. He'd never been a man to take chances. If that *hombre* ahead was running from something, could be he would try and pull some trick or other.

But now close up Simpson decided the man looked dead, or unconscious. He unhooked his spare canteen off the saddle horn and dismounted. A cursory examination of the prone figure told him he was a tall man and wiry with it. Well, he had to see what he could do, though he didn't hold out much hope.

He reached for the man's shoulder and turned him over only to look into a youthful face and a pair of blue eyes that were crinkled at the corners and dancing with amusement. No desperation, no strain in those orbs at all. They were staring straight back into his now hard stare. But before he could react Simpson felt the cold, round bore of a Colt .45 being jabbed into his gut.

'Saw you comin', mister,' the stranger said. He grinned some more.

Instantly, Simpson's stomach tightened. A rime of anger spread swiftly through him. 'Why, you no-good sonofabitch,' he breathed. 'I came here aimin' to help you.'

The youth looked almost apologetic. 'Well, I can only thank you for that,' he said, then shrugged, 'but needs of the day, you understand ...'

'Needs of the day be damned!' rasped Simpson, scowling.

Even as he spoke Simpson felt his side gun being removed from its holster, then tossed into the brush behind him. 'Back off just a little, mister,' the stranger instructed. 'But leave the canteen.'

Growling his displeasure at being so comprehensively duped, Simpson complied. Standing some dozen yards back he said bitterly, 'You think you're goin' to get away with this?'

The young man moistened his lips first then took a grateful swallow from the canteen and wiped his mouth with the back of his hand. 'Figure it this way: I could damn well kill you an' that would

solve just about everythin' between you an'
me, pronto.'

Simpson's stare grew steely. He gazed
into the blue eyes looking up at him, still
with that impish amusement in them. It
surprised him to find, though, amid that
easy-going stare there was some sympathy,
too. *For the plight Simpson now found
himself in?*

But the Colt, held steady in the stranger's
bony hand, said that could be a false
assumption.

Simpson said, 'I repeat: I came to help,
mister. There's no need for this.'

The man took another long swig from
the canteen, waved the Colt, smiled again
before pursing his lips, then said, 'Don't
think I ain't grateful. But, as I said,
the needs of the day force me to be
ungracious.'

That last line told Simpson the man had
maybe had a little education at some time,
not that it would help any here.

'The roan will carry the two of us,' he

pointed out, a little desperately. 'No need for this.'

The young man got to his feet. He was over six feet tall and whipcord slim. 'It's a fine-looking beast and you're probably right,' he admitted. 'But I have to move fast. There was a misunderstanding back up the trail I'm eager to get away from.'

Without bothering to explain more and with catlike agility the man swung into the saddle on the roan. Simpson watched him untie his blanket roll, unhook the two saddle-bags with his possibles in them and throw them down. Then the stranger followed them with the saddle Simpson had rescued back up the trail, but retained the Spencer.

'Ain't the time right now to change saddles,' he explained. 'An' I want the horse to carry as little weight as possible.'

'You're puttin' me in a bad spot here,' Simpson said tightly. 'I ain't usually a forgivin' man.'

'Don't think I ain't regretful 'bout what

I'm doin',' the man returned. 'But I figure help'll be along pretty soon, so you won't be inconvenienced for too long.'

He unhooked the spare canteen and dropped it to the ground. 'That's just to prove I ain't the complete sonofabitch you're now maybe thinkin' I am.' He grinned again and waved a carefree hand. '*Adios amigo.*'

He swung the roan and headed across the flats. At maybe two hundred yards he reined again. Simpson watched him toss down his Winchester. 'A handsome piece,' he yelled before he urged the horse on again.

Fuming, Simpson gazed after the train of dust that indicated the man's swift passage across the burning land. Now he cursed loudly and kicked at a startled gecko, missed. He'd been took, fair and square. And he figured the town of Hell to be at least another twelve miles ahead, although he wasn't sure. Any which way, though, it was going to be a long and weary walk.

But what did the man mean when he said help should be along shortly ...?

Simpson found he was in no mood to speculate. He searched for and found his Colt, checked the mechanism and put it back in its holster. He tied his roll to the stranger's saddle as best he could, took a swig from the canteen he'd left behind, then humped up the saddle—he'd sell the damned thing first chance he had, or use it—and set to walking, stopping only to retrieve his Winchester.

He saw the column of dust behind him about an hour later. He had stopped to drink from the canteen, to mop his brow and to ease his aching limbs after carrying the dumped equipment for so long.

He sat down on the saddle and waited. A few minutes later the posse of men hauled rein in a cloud of dust around him. Simpson counted five—trail-worn and angry at being so, it appeared. Well, the sonofabitch had said they'd be along.

'Howdy,' he said, with a levity he didn't

feel. He knew he must look a dumb damned fool sitting there.

The thick-set, hard-bitten-looking one in the lead said, 'You run into Taw McAdam?'

Simpson described the man who had set him afoot. 'That him?' he said when he'd finished.

The leader nodded fiercely. 'That's him.'

'He wanted for somethin'?' pursued Simpson.

'He molested my daughter,' rapped the reply. 'No man can do that to mine.'

'You saw him kiss her is all, Abel,' growled a tall, lean man in the pack behind. 'Ain't no law agin sparkin' a girl. It's as old as Adam, that kind of thing.' Simpson noticed the fellow didn't attempt to hide the weariness in his voice.

'Did I ask you for an opinion, Lew?' roared the lead man. 'I don't want his filthy hands on her, y'hear?'

It was becoming clear to Simpson that this man ran the outfit.

15

'What do you aim to do when you catch him?' he asked, blandly.

'I've a mind to string him up,' barked the reply. 'Will do, maybe.'

'For courtin' a girl?' Simpson narrowed his eyelids. 'What kind of damned country is this?'

He became aware the lead man's tawny gaze was now bearing down on him from the height sitting the big chestnut gelding gave him. It was a ferocious stare. 'You wantin' to buy in on this?' he rasped.

Simpson shook his head. 'Hell, no. I got scores of my own to settle with that sonofabitch. I just figure kissin' a girl ain't exactly a hangin' offence, that's all.'

'You do, huh? Well, maybe you've figured wrong in this case.' The leader turned to the men behind him. 'OK. Let's git. We're wastin' time here.'

The posse of men hesitated a moment, exchanged glances. 'How about the stranger?' said Lew, the one who had spoken previously.

The tawny-eyed leader said, as if surprised, 'What about him?'

'Ain't we givin' him a stirrup?'

'Hell is eight miles up ahead,' growled the leader. 'Way I figure it, if he was damned fool enough to get himself into this mess, let him walk his way out of it. Maybe teach him a lesson.'

'Now hold on, mister,' protested Simpson. He stepped forward aggressively. 'What kind of people are you—leavin' a man out in the desert like this?'

'The sort of people that don't git themselves into that kind of trouble in the first place,' growled the burly leader. That brought guffaws from the crew behind him. But the man added, grudgingly, 'You appear able. I reckon you'll live. Come on, boys.'

'Damn you,' roared Simpson, shaking his fist as he watched them ride off into the sage that was beginning to sprout ahead.

It was dark when Simpson hit the one

street of Hell. It didn't cause much of a stir. Most places were shut up for the night. He'd already decided the town was well named for he'd gone through a form of purgatory just to reach it, and looked as though he had. His lips were cracked and bleeding, his skin raw because of the constant battering from the sun, despite his wide-brimmed hat. The large patches of sweat on his dark-blue shirt were thickly etched with salt-white. It was only his iron will, bodily fitness and anger at being put in this position that had kept him plodding on, almost without pause all those weary mess of miles it took to get here.

The sign on the saloon he stopped in front of announced it was Satan's Lair. It caused a wry, if painful, grin to form on his thin, cracked lips. Despite all, he found he hadn't quite lost his sense of humour, though it hurt like that dark deity's traditional home to attempt the smile.

He stepped into the welcoming yellow

kerosene lamplight. As he walked towards the bar the 'keeper stared at him, as did the rest of the company in the drinking house. The buzz of talk dropped abruptly. Simpson thought little of it. It was only what he could expect, being a stranger in town and in this condition.

At the bar he dumped his baggage and said, 'A large, cold beer.'

'Coming up.' The 'keep's stare was neutral as it stayed on him. To Simpson it was as though his sudden dusty and sweat-rimmed appearance here was something the barman saw coming through the door every day of the week. But the 'keep added unnecessarily, 'You walk in?'

A titter came from behind, somewhere in the gloom.

Though still sizzling with anger, Simpson ignored the damn-fool question for now, and the reaction to it. There were certain priorities to be met first. 'Just give me the beer,' he said tiredly, but gingerly, for it hurt his throat to talk.

He paid for the schooner of amber liquid and drank long and gratefully. He'd ordered and drunk another before the enquiry came from the table close by, 'You managed the hike OK, huh? Haw, haw, haw.' More guffaws followed.

Simpson lifted his gaze slowly and turned.

The five of them were sat around a table nearby, pasteboards and shotglasses containing varying quantities of drink covering its smooth surface. Clearly, they were in the middle of a card game. The thick-set one was grinning at him—the one that had headed the posse that was running after Taw McAdam.

'Well, well,' purred Simpson, but the easy-going sound gave lie to the iron-hard anger in him. 'Look who we have here. I was kind of hopin' I'd run into you boys.'

He moved across the space between them with deceptive speed. He took a bunch of the spokesman's shirt, up near the collar. Before anyone could move—the surprise had been so complete—Simpson was hoisting the man to his feet. He then swung him around and hit him full in the mouth before the man could put up any semblance of a defence.

The punch sent the *hombre* clattering back across the space between the bar and the table. He hit the edge of the mahogany top hard. The force of the impact drove the wind out of him in a harsh gasp.

Simpson followed up swiftly, smacking his left fist deep into the man's gut, folding him over. Then he brought up his right, short and brisk, the whole weight of his big body behind it. It snapped the man's head back. He cried out as he rolled off the edge of the bar and crashed to the floor. He tried to rise then slumped, out cold.

Almost immediately and with howls of anger, the rest of the men seated around the table rose and came pounding over to him. Simpson found himself immediately swamped with bodies, all swinging hard blows.

As he lashed out with iron fists he heard somebody nearby bawl urgently, 'Fetch the marshal!', but it was near lost to Simpson in the flurries of flailing fists he was now desperately trying to defend himself from.

Then, through the fight-red mists before his eyes, he saw the chair. He grabbed and swung it massively around him, feeling it connect twice before somebody had him round the waist. Soon more range-hardened hands began bearing him to the floor. Then more blows rained down on him, causing him to grunt with pain before the boom of a Colt and a harsh voice calling, 'That's enough, boys,' brought matters abruptly to a close.

After moments and dizzy from the barrage of punches he'd received, Simpson rose slowly and stood in the middle of the barroom floor, shaking his shaggy head in an attempt to clear the muzziness in it.

'Now what in the hell is goin' on here?'

demanded Marshal John Patter slowly, tiredly.

Simpson gazed through already swelling eyelids at the serious-eyed, stocky, round-faced lawman, standing feet apart in the middle of the barroom floor. A Colt was held firm in his right hand.

'Just settlin' a small dispute,' Simpson mouthed through cut and bloody lips.

'Like hell,' growled one of the crew that had been at the card table. He was sagging and bleeding from a cut high on his forehead. 'He just upped an' started beatin' the shit outa Mr Cross here.'

The puncher waved a paw towards the thick-set *hombre* now groaning and rising from the floor, shaking a bloody, craggy head that Simpson could see was covered with greying sandy hair, now his hat had been jolted off his head.

Simpson met the marshal's pale stare as he turned back to him. 'You have a reason to do that?' Patter demanded.

Simpson explained.

Abel Cross, owner of the Circle C in the foothills east of Hell, was now on his feet and glowering venomously at Carl. 'I want him jailed, John,' he stormed, waving a gnarled, plump finger. 'Assault an' battery. No arguments.'

John Patter nodded. 'Yup,' he said. 'Guess that fits the bill, despite the provocation.'

Simpson gazed steadily at the lawman, while trying to ignore his throbbing hurts. 'You agree there was provocation, then?' he rasped bitterly.

Patter waved the Colt. 'I jest said, didn't I? Even so, mister—move. Your behaviour has booked you a night's lodgin's in Hell's calaboose.'

Simpson winced as he gingerly felt the lump rising on the side of his head. But the words sent sudden rage surging up in him. 'Well damn you,' he stormed, 'I was left afoot! In the desert! What kind of law have you got here that's able to condone that?'

'The kind that keeps things quiet,' said Patter. 'That do?'

'Well to hell with it,' growled Simpson. 'What sort of damned justice is it that stops a man rightin' a wrong done to him?'

Patter tugged thoughtfully at the thick, dark moustache on his upper lip, then frowned. 'I was just goin' to keep you in hoosegow overnight, to cool down, mister,' he said at length. 'Now, fer all your arguin' an' your obviously bad disposition, I figure you maybe need another two days.'

Simpson stared, outraged. 'Dag blast it, that ain't fair,' he roared. 'What about Taw McAdam? He stole my hoss, put me afoot. That's a hangin' offence where I come from.'

'A fine big roan?' Patter said, ignoring the suggestion of a lynching. 'A Texas saddle on it?'

'That's it,' rasped Simpson. 'You seen it?'

'Taw said he'd borrowed it,' explained Patter. 'Said you'd be through to collect.

25

He left it in the livery stable with orders to have it curried and oat-fed 'til you got here.'

'The damned gall!' roared Simpson. 'He live around here?'

'His pa owns the M-M spread on the west range.'

Simpson swung on Abel Cross, who was still glowering at him while mopping blood from his mashed lips. Simpson pointed at him accusingly. 'Well, that sonofabitch and his crew were out to lynch him,' he roared. 'What are you goin' to do about that?'

Marshal Patter smiled indulgently. 'Nothin'. Abel gets just a little worked up about things sometimes,' he said evenly. 'He'll cool down. Nothin' to heed.'

'Nothin' to heed!' snorted Simpson. 'An' you're jailin' me fer hittin' a man that deserved to be hit—a man that left me out in the desert to die?'

The lawman nodded. 'Beyond the exaggeration of you dyin' out there, that sizes it up, you bein' a stranger hereabouts.'

Simpson now felt Patter's Colt jam in his gut, and his own being removed from its holster. 'Now move, mister,' the marshal said, 'I've spent too much time explainin'.'

More guffaws came—from all directions this time. Simpson glowered around him, at the leering faces etched in the amber lamplight before turning back to Patter. 'I was aimin' to pass through this territory peaceably, mister,' he gritted, feeling his penchant for fair play was taking a serious battering here. 'Now I gotta growing urge to stay awhile.'

The marshal raised dark, bushy brows. 'Mister, that wouldn't be wise.'

Simpson glowered coldly. 'I'll judge what's wise for me, an' what ain't. You got that, lawman?'

Patter's brown gaze hardened. 'Now don't get too uppity with me, mister. I'm doin' you a favour. By the way, you got a name—just for the record?'

'Sure, I got a name. Carl Simpson.' Meanly, the ex-lawman stared into the yellow gloom around him and at the pale faces surrounding him in the long, narrow saloon. 'An' you'd better remember it.'

Abel Cross paced forward angrily, until he was no more than a couple of feet from Simpson's tall, well-built body. 'Why, you sonofabitch! You threatenin' *me* among all that?'

Simpson returned the hot glare. 'You in particular. So from now on move light around me, Cross. Move light.'

His face now red-purple, his anger flaring, Cross went for his Colt. 'Goddamn you. Why, I oughta ...'

Marshal Patter cocked his own hand gun, aimed it at the Circle C owner. 'Cool it, Abel. I know this man's name and if you called him out you wouldn't have a prayer. But be assured, he's leavin' the territory. I'll see to it personal. Soon as he done his time an' thunk about what he's gettin' into when I've explained it to him, he'll see things different. I almost guarantee it.'

Growling, Cross slowly replaced his Colt, his temper clearly cooling. 'Well, see as you do, John. Just see as you do.' He turned to his hands. 'Come on, boys. We got a game of poker to finish. Guess we can forgit Taw McAdam for now. There'll come a day for him.'

TWO

Simpson stared up at the jail window. It was a small square with iron bars set close. Through them a shaft of moonlight was spearing, etching lines on the opposite wall. Marshal Patter had fed him when he had protested he hadn't eaten since early morning. Now replete, Simpson sat on the iron-frame bed feeling moody and miserable and nursing his hurts. He didn't quite know which bruise to explore first. Even though Marshal Patter confessed to knowing his past in Ladderet, he hadn't paid any particular deference to it, not that Simpson wanted him to. That part of his life had been dead three years. He wanted it left that way.

But, damn it, what was he doing here? Feeling mean he rocked morosely and felt his barked knuckles. All he had been doing was riding across this lousy basin, heading for California. Now this.

'Pssst ... Mr Simpson?' The call came from outside and it had Simpson straightening out of his slump of misery immediately. A chuckle followed it, then an addition to the man's first words, *'Welcome to Hell!'*

Fully alert, Simpson cocked his head, made sour and angry by the jaunty humour he was being confronted with. Nevertheless, he climbed on to the bunk and peered out into the dirty, weed-filled alley beyond. Imaged in the moonlight he saw Taw McAdam grinning up at him, his lean, young face creased, his blue eyes merry.

Simpson felt his gut tauten. He clenched the iron bars. 'Why, you low-down sonofabitch—you come to gloat?'

Looking hurt, McAdam cut air with a bony, long-fingered hand. 'Hell no,' he whispered. 'Though I deserve all the foul words you can put your tongue to, I guess.

31

But say 'em quiet. Thing is I come to get you out, Mr Simpson. Figure that's the least I can do, seein' as how I got you into this mess in the first place.'

'You've *what?*' Simpson stared incredulously at the grinning figure in the alley. 'An' how d'you know my name?'

Looking surprised to be asked, McAdam said, 'Why, it's on your saddle.' But Simpson saw it didn't seem to mean a lot to the young man. Instead McAdam "shushed" and said, 'So quiet! Here, catch a hold of this chain. Draw it through the bars, pass me the two ends.'

Recovering quickly from his surprise and not in the mood to question his change of fortunes, Simpson did as he was bid. Whatever was between himself and Taw McAdam could wait.

Gathering the chain, McAdam wrapped it round the saddle horn of the pinto waiting in the shadows, along with, Simpson now noticed, his own saddled roan. The chain secured, McAdam urged the pinto on. The links tensed, quivered as McAdam's horse took up the slack and strained forward.

Quietly urging the pinto to greater efforts, McAdam nevertheless used the quirt around his wrist as well. The cement holding the bars, it soon became clear, was not of the best quality and began to crumble almost immediately. Soon they were ripped out of the adobe and Simpson scrambled swiftly through the hole into the cool night. He quickly mounted the roan.

Impatiently he watched McAdam unwrap the chain from the saddle horn and sling it across the pinto's withers and climb up. Then turning the youth said, 'Follow me.'

Still not questioning it, Simpson did as he was bid. Soon they were out into the sage, heading west.

Two miles out of Hell, McAdam tugged rein and turned. Simpson could see he had that damned grin on his face again.

He watched McAdam begin fumbling

in his coat pocket. To Simpson's surprise the youth pulled out what he saw was his own Colt. McAdam held it out towards him. Simpson took it. The moon was big enough to allow him to clearly see his initials, CS, carved into the ivory handle. The last time he had seen the weapon, Marshal John Patter had been placing it in a drawer of his office desk. Now McAdam drew a Winchester out of his saddle scabbard. Simpson could tell immediately that that was his, too. McAdam passed it over.

'How in the hell did you get these?' Simpson rasped.

McAdam grinned even more widely. 'Now an' agin, ol' Marshal John likes to sleep in a real bed at nights, instead of the bunk in his office,' he informed him mischievously. 'Preferably Sadie Jameson's bed. A female of his acquaintance, of course. Well, I watched him while he made off for that dear lady's place, then well, the lock on the marshal's office don't take that much pickin', so I picked it.'

'Why in the name of Christ didn't you get the cell keys while you were at it?' demanded Simpson. 'Save pullin' the damned bars out.'

'I would have, on'y ol' John took 'em with him,' said McAdam. He added protestingly, 'Damn it, he ain't *that* dumb.'

Slightly exasperated, Simpson glared across the space between himself and Taw McAdam. What in tarnation do you do with a young hothead like this? First he takes your horse, then he breaks you out of jail.

He climbed down off the roan, shook his head. 'So now you figure gettin' me out of jail an' gittin' my guns squares us, huh?' he grunted.

From his pinto's back, McAdam stared incredulously down at him. 'Well, don't it?'

'No, not in a prairie mile it don't,' snorted Simpson. 'An' for one plain reason.

If you hadn't taken my hoss I would have had no need to hit Cross ...'

McAdam's gleeful whoop cut across his words before he warbled, 'You hit Abel Cross?' As if delighted he yanked off his hat and swung it above his head, whooped again. Then he said, 'By golly, you sure is provin' to be a rooster, mister!' His gaze gleamed happily in the moonlight.

Bearing the exultant interruption, Simpson went on sourly, '... an' if I hadn't had cause to do that, I would have been nigh on out of this basin by now, had I had a mind to give Hell a miss.'

'Why *did* you hit him?' urged McAdam eagerly, still delighted. 'I gotta know.'

'He left me to walk in,' Simpson said, but resenting the joy hitting Cross had given McAdam.

'He *what?*' ejaculated McAdam, his smile melting abruptly, his sandy brows rising. 'Why that low-down sonof—'

Simpson raised a staying hand. 'Whoa ... just hold it, mister,' he growled bitterly.

'I seem to recall somebody else doin' that self same thing.'

'Hell,' protested MacAdam, 'I had good reason. He didn't.'

'He seemed to think he had,' said Simpson. 'But when I got to town and disputed that supposition I finished up in jail.'

'Yeah, well, saw Patter takin' you across the street,' said McAdam, a little sheepishly. 'But I didn't know why. Jus' got you out 'cos I figured I owed you.'

Simpson nodded grimly. Had he not been feeling so sore—physically as well as mentally—about the whole business, he might have seen the funny side of it, perhaps put it down to one of life's vagaries, but at the moment he found he couldn't. This young man needed a lesson taught and, by God, he was going to teach it!

'Git down off that horse, Taw,' he said. 'I aim to whup you good. An' maybe you'll think twice next time about puttin' a man afoot in the desert.'

Young McAdam shrugged, hesitated a moment before climbing uncertainly down from his pinto. 'You're beat up some already. You full sure about this, Mr Simpson?'

Carl nodded soberly. 'You can bet your damned boots I am, boy.' He set up his fists. 'But I'll play it by the Marquess of Queensberry's rules.'

MacAdam stared at him. 'Now who in the hell is *that?*'

Simpson stared. 'You don't know?'

McAdam shook his towhead. 'Wouldn't be askin' if I did. Ranch style's the on'y way I know. My pa, Brad McAdam, showed me how to do that. Though I figure it ain't right to use the spurs.'

Faced with such ignorance regarding the rules of pugilism, Simpson nodded. 'OK, boy! Ranch style. An' if you got a thing about the spurs we'll take 'em off.' He bent and commenced unstrapping his rowels.

Reflecting on it later, Simpson figured

he should have known better than to give whom he thought to be a wet-eared boy every chance, counting all the fierce barroom brawls he'd been in, but he had been able to roll away just in time as McAdam's right boot came swinging towards his jaw. However, despite his brisk evasion, it had thumped into his shoulder with enough force to send him sprawling into the dust and crying out with the pain of it.

Scrambling to his feet and glaring he roared, 'Damn it. I weren't ready. You said no spurs.'

MacAdam shrugged. 'I said I figured it weren't *right* to use spurs, but didn't say take 'em off. You figured to do that.'

'I'm tryin' to meet you fair an' square, boy,' snarled Simpson. 'You're sure putting the down on that, by God. It's all horn an' hoof now.'

Taw McAdam shrugged again. 'Pa allus said that in a ruckus every man should look out for himself, though he should fall short of stompin' a man to death,' explained McAdam. That damned grin spread across his lean face once more.

'He did, huh, boy?' said Simpson. 'So let's take his advice.'

He scooped up a handful of dust and threw it. It billowed into Taw's face. Though the youth fended it off with a hastily raised arm, it diverted his attention enough.

Taking his advantage Simpson roared in, first driving his left into McAdam's gut, then swinging his right into his face. It was his favourite manoeuvre. Taw staggered back, driven by the force of the blows and sprawled on to the ground. Simpson followed up eagerly, raising a large right boot. Seeing him coming Taw rolled away desperately before scrambling to his feet.

'Pa said no stompin',' he protested hotly.

'To hell with that, boy,' countered Simpson.

He was happy to see he'd wiped the grin off the boy's face but he wasn't ready for Taw as he came boring in like a bull that had gone berserk. His tow-haired head hammered into Simpson's flat, hard stomach, driving the wind out of him in a retching gasp. It was then Simpson realized McAdam was as tall as he was and that his lean body was as hard-muscled as his own and clearly rawhide tough.

Urgently, Simpson grasped the young man's coat as he went down, pulling him with him and drove his knee up, deep into his groin. It was Taw's turn to let out an agonized noise. Not hesitating, Simpson butted McAdam's nose this time with his hard forehead, but as he did he felt Taw's boot driving into his private parts.

Simpson found the pain was exquisite. It rampaged through him like fire, causing him to release Taw, get up and stagger around holding on to those fragile, injured extremities.

When he was able to concentrate again—which had to be quick, judging by the boy's performance up until now—he stared around, looking for the next direction McAdam was going to come from. But he saw the boy grinning at him and standing off.

'I asked you if you were sure about this, Mr Simpson,' he said, as though he already figured the opposition mediocre and the contest won. 'Is you?'

'Damn you, boy, I've on'y just started,' Simpson roared. 'You come on in an' take your medicine right now.'

Taw shook his head. 'Pa said I should let my opponent come on in to me,' he said.

'He did, huh?' growled Simpson. 'Well, then, in that case—here I come, kid.'

He rushed in, hoping to take the McAdam boy unawares. He didn't. He ran into a hard-knuckled right that looped in from nowhere and jarred into the side of his head. But he kept lunging in, using just brute force. He hammered his way through Taw's defence and began crashing blows into the youth's body. But he was getting a fair measure of punishment in return. This Taw McAdam was no stranger to a rough and tumble. And for sure, he wasn't a boy, he was a man grown. In body and fighting knowledge, anyway.

Breath rasping hard from him now, Simpson continued to ram in blow after blow only to be met with equal treatment. Finally they split apart. Like spent bulls, they both stood staring at each other through the silver light of the moon, breath being gulped in with matched urgency, blood seeping from numerous cuts and abrasions.

'You had enough, boy?' Simpson gasped after moments.

Taw grinned with bloody lips, but stared, dazed. He had to gulp in more air before he could answer. 'Was jus' figurin' on askin' you the same question, Mr Simpson,' he finally panted.

Slightly startled by that, for he thought he'd done enough, Simpson growled, 'You were? God damn it, boy, you take some convincin'.'

But when he'd drawn in more air he began to laugh, though it hurt like fury to do it. He couldn't help it. There was a certain irony in the situation and something about the boy a man had to like. Taw McAdam began to laugh, too. In the end they both finished up rolling on the ground and roaring with hilarity, though Simpson thought it a crazy reaction to have, being twenty-four years of age and an ex-lawman.

When their merriment finally subsided Simpson said, 'Well, I got to hand it to you. You pack a mean punch.'

McAdam grinned back at him through cut lips. He wiped a hand down his dust-caked jeans and extended it. Simpson took it readily. 'Guess you ain't no slouch yourself, Mr Simpson, comin' right down to it,' he said. There was companionable silence between them for a moment, then Taw became fully serious. He squinted across the space between them. 'What you aimin' to do now?'

Finally calmed Simpson found the matter didn't need much thought. He figured he'd squared off the wrongs he'd been dealt in this basin and there was no need to pursue them further. 'Ride on, I guess,' he said. 'I ain't keen on the hospitality I've received around here so far.'

'Figure Pa might like to meet you afore you go,' said McAdam. 'There'll be a ranch-style breakfast in it for you,' he added, 'help you on your way. Reckon I owe you that much.'

'You paid most of your debt, boy,' said Simpson, 'gettin' me out of that hoosegow. But I could use some travellin' vittles. I was aimin' to pick those up in Hell.'

McAdam grinned. 'I guess the M-M can take care of that, too.'

Feeling sudden warm comradeship now, Simpson nodded. 'Well, that sounds fine to me.'

Simpson climbed wearily into the saddle. When Taw had climbed up as well he said, 'So lead on, partner.'

Taw McAdam grinned across at him before he headed the pinto out on to the moonlit range. Simpson swung the big roan in alongside him and they rode in friendly silence.

THREE

They'd left the drier country three miles back and pink dawn was cracking the eastern horizon when Simpson and Taw McAdam topped the rise overlooking the M-M buildings. By the bend in the creek, at the base of the long slope, Simpson saw amongst the cottonwoods down there, a long, low adobe ranch-house. Men were already moving about getting ready to tackle the chores of the day. Clustered around the house he observed other constructions: a bunkhouse, barns and lodgepole corrals. Smoke was rising from a metal stack, back of the ranch-house.

'Seems Ma's gittin' breakfast,' Taw said, with a grin. 'Come on.' He urged his horse down the last of the slope.

After both had seen to their horses,

Simpson followed Taw into the ranch-house. It was a big common room they entered with range regalia freely decorating the walls. A tall, stringy man with bow legs and a sagging moustache came out of one of the rooms off immediately they entered.

'You been out to the Circle C agin, boy, sparkin' Lucy Cross?' he barked right off. His faded eyes stared out from range-narrowed eyelids. 'You know you got duties to attend to here.'

'Jest called to pay my respects, Pa.' Taw rubbed his nose, a look of injured innocence on his face. 'I'll git my chores done. No need for sleep.'

Brad McAdam nodded, but complained, 'Well, you know what Abel thinks about you goin' over there.'

Taw looked indignant. 'Dang it, he can't wrap her in cottonwool for ever. I reckon a man has a right to spark the girl of his choosin'. Can't understand why Mr Cross gets so all fired up about it.'

Old man McAdam continued to stare. 'You can't? More'n once I've told you. Gittin' sick of tellin' you, but I'll detail it once more. Clarissa, the daughter Abel had by his first wife, you recall? She ran off with that no-good gamblin' man from Carolina? Finished up pregnant and abandoned, then was finally found dead, along with her baby boy, in a San Francisco slum? You remember that?' Without waiting for an answer, McAdam went on. 'It was said she was too proud to ask for help an' died of a broken heart. Well, when Abe heard about it, it damn near broke him, I can tell you. He thought the sun shone out o' that girl.' Brad McAdam gestured impatiently now. 'So use your brain, will you, son? You've tried awful hard recently to pass yourself off as a wild boy. Is it any wonder Abel don't put any trust in you?'

Taw snorted. 'Aw, that's just high spirits, Pa. You've allus said a man has to get that out of his system afore he settled down. An', sure as hell, I ain't no Mississippi gamblin' sonofabitch!'

Brad McAdam growled and shuffled uncomfortably. 'Maybe I have said that, maybe I ain't, but it don't say you have to take my advice, does it!' It seemed to sour the older McAdam a little to admit he may have advised Taw on sowing his wild oats. As if to cover that indiscretion he snorted, 'An', dang it, just you watch your language around the house. I won't have it. It offends your mother greatly.' Now Simpson became aware Brad McAdam's gaze had switched to himself. 'That out of the way ... who's your friend, son?'

Taw said, as if eager to get off the subject of Lucy Cross, 'This is Carl Simpson, Pa. We, er, kind of met up yesterday. Brung him in for breakfast. He's in need of a few trail vittles, too.'

Old man McAdam leaned forward. His worn features screwed up enquiringly. 'Would the state of both your faces be a result of that meetin'?'

Uncomfortably, Simpson glanced at Taw. The young man's right eye was purple, swollen until it was nearly closed. There was a cut on his forehead. His lips were badly bruised and there was a lump on the side of his jaw. Simpson ran a self-conscious hand over his own battered features. God knew what he looked like, for he'd had Abel Cross's boys work him over, as well as Taw.

During Simpson's scrutiny, Taw had been shuffling and looking sheepishly at his father. 'Well, there was a slight difference of opinion about a certain matter,' he admitted.

Old man McAdam's look became serious, though there was a hint of veiled amusement, or resignation, there as well. He shot his bushy eyebrows up and momentarily preened his stringy moustache, as if thoughtfully. 'Well, you'd better spit it all out, son,' he said at length. 'Don't like to get to know things second hand, you know that.'

Taw tried to sniff up partly blood-blocked nostrils. Simpson caught the boy's swift, almost apologetic glance before he went on to trot out every true detail.

When it was told old man McAdam nodded. 'You left this man in the desert an' Abel threatened to hang you agin?'

'Pa, you know he don't mean that, not for real,' protested Taw.

Brad McAdam's look was doubtful. 'He can be an impulsive man, can Abel. An' because of what happened to Clarissa, I wouldn't live in certainty of that.'

'But that'd be murder!' spouted Taw.

'Wouldn't be to Abel,' said old man McAdam. 'He'll figure he's protectin' his own.'

Taw wailed, 'But I love her, Pa! Why is he so unreasonable?'

Brad McAdam growled, 'I've told you why, boy. You'll just have to prove yourself more worthy than that no-good gambler an' convince Abel you are. Maybe that old mossy horn'll relent when you do.'

'How do I do that?' moaned Taw.

Old man McAdam gazed hard at his son before he shot up his greying brows. 'That's the dilemma you're in, boy. It's up to you to start an' grow up an' figure a way around it, if you're goin' to win your lady.'

A small, middle-aged woman with sun-bleached blonde hair streaked with grey and set in ringlets came in carrying a plate of flapjacks and set them upon the big table established in the light near the far window.

'Been listen',' she said in a calm, but stern voice. 'Your pa's right, Taw. Heed him.'

Simpson became aware now that Mrs Flora McAdam's gaze was on him. He swept off his battered hat in respect of her sudden presence. 'If Brad ain't yet, I would like to thank you, Mr Simpson, for sparing my boy after he took your horse in the desert,' she said. 'I've known men be gunned down for far less than that. And you were right to thrash him. So you're doubly welcome to our table. However, I would like both you boys to wash up first. Water's already waitin' out the back.'

Simpson bowed slightly, but he was in doubt about the thrashing. 'Gracious of you, ma'am. I thank you.'

Outside, he and Taw stripped to the waist at the wash bench. Both winced as the effort fired their bodily bruises into fresh pain. However, Simpson found the early morning rays of the sun were welcome on his broad, well-muscled, but punished back, though the water and carbolic soap stung with new fury as they came in contact with his battered torso. He then fished out his cut-throat razor from his possibles and with extreme care not to further damage his already scarred face, using the piece of broken mirror already propped above the wooden trough, scraped off two days of beard before shucking into his clean change of clothes. He recalled with affection that his own mother had been a stickler for cleanliness at the table, too.

Once more in the common room they sat down to syrup and flapjacks, ham and a platter of fried eggs and ate hungrily and almost silently. Finally replete, Simpson said, as Mrs McAdam came bustling in to clear the table, 'That sure filled a need and I thank you most heartily, ma'am, and, of course, you too, sir.' He gazed across the table into old man McAdam's long, weather-beaten features, his grey, steady eyes that now studied him. While they had eaten breakfast the elder McAdam had been sitting apart from them, puffing his pipe reflectively, having already eaten.

The old man nodded, accepting his gratitude. 'So where are you headin' for now, Mr Simpson?' he said conversationally.

'I had California in mind,' Carl said.

Brad McAdam cleared his throat. 'I've heard there is plenty of opportunity there. But you look a saddleman.'

'Shouldn't stop a man,' pointed out

Simpson. 'Change can be good.'

Now McAdam knitted his greying brows together, as if remembering some long-past event. 'Carl Simpson ... that name's been jinglin' somethin' at the back of my mind.'

Simpson felt a sinking feeling. *There was always somebody who had a jingle in the back of their mind.* 'In case your memory comes full back, that was long ago, Mr McAdam. I ain't cleaned up a town in years.'

McAdam's eyes lit up. He pointed the tobacco-stained stem of his pipe. 'Con Valley war ... town of Ladderet ... Territorial Marshal Carl Simpson ... stood alone against the three Mosten boys in the final showdown ...'

Simpson pursed his battered lips. 'Three years ago, Mr McAdam,' he said. 'An eight-year-old boy was also killed in the fracas. At that point I figured ... well ...' Simpson let his voice drift into silence for a moment as the pang of pain and regret for the past renewed itself. Then he sighed.

'Well, it was an awful thing to happen.'

Old man McAdam coughed as if slightly embarrassed, nodded soberly. 'Heard about that, too. Terrible business, to be sure.' Then he added, as if to offer consolation, 'But the news sheet said no blame was laid at your door, not even by the boy's parents.'

'True,' admitted Simpson. 'But a lot of lead flew that day. It could have been me that done it. What made it worse was ... well, that boy was my godson. So help me, I bought him his first bible.'

Old man McAdam's face became grave. Sympathy filled his gaze. 'I guess such a thing as that can be awful hard to come to terms with.'

Simpson took a deep breath, strove to bury the ghosts he found were once more rearing up in his mind. 'I'd like to change the subject, sir. The past is dead. I don't want to resurrect it.'

Brad McAdam rose, stepped forward and tapped the dottle out of his pipe into the empty bean can on the table. 'I respect that. I shouldn't have brought it up.' Stuffing his pipe in his pocket he unhooked his tall-crowned hat from the spread of antlers on the wall behind him and pulled it on. 'Well, a ranch don't run itself,' he said. He turned to Taw. 'I want you in the saddle in ten minutes, boy.' Then he switched his grey look back to Simpson and pushed out a big, sinewy hand. Simpson took it. He found McAdam's press was firm and friendly. 'I'll ask Ma to see to your needs, Mr Simpson,' McAdam went on. 'And, in case I ain't here when you go, I wish you a safe journey.'

Before Simpson could properly thank him in return, on bowlegs, old man McAdam briskly ambled out the door Mrs McAdam had exited through after she'd cleared the table.

'Though I know nothin' of what Pa said—wow,' breathed Taw after he'd gone, 'a real live shootin' lawman? Hell, Carl, you should've said.'

Simpson smiled a painful smile. 'Would it have made a difference?'

'It might have.'

'Well, I don't want it to, Taw. I want Ladderet forgotten.'

Young McAdam shrugged. 'OK, if you want. You're leavin' anyway, so it don't matter much, I guess. But I'd be real proud if you'd stay awhile. Things on this range ain't exactly hunky-dory right now. I'm sure Pa would go along with it.'

Simpson rose from the table. 'I've had a bellyful of other people's troubles, Taw, over the years. I reckon you an' your pa'll make out. You'd best git on now, like your pa said. An' if I don't see you agin ...'

He made to extend his hand but yells from outside brought the conversation to an abrupt halt. With Taw he crossed the big common room. Out on the stoop they watched the twelve riders crossing the broad pastures of grama grass, fed by creeks from bountiful springs in the two canyons which were orange-walled chasms cutting into the pine-topped mesas five miles north, before opening out on to M-M range.

Standing beside Taw, Simpson heard the youngster suck in air. His youthful face set grim. 'Bart Tranter,' he breathed. 'Now what in the hell does he want?'

As he spoke old man McAdam came round the edge of the ranch-house from the rear. He joined them. He stared hard at Taw. 'Keep a rein on your temper, son. We'll hear what he has to say.'

'Ellis Canyon is ours, Pa,' gritted Taw. 'He's no right to keep on about it.'

Though old man McAdam nodded agreement he said, 'Leave the talkin' to me. Right now, I guess he has more than just the water in Ellis Canyon on his mind. While you were gone, I strung wire across the north access.'

Taw stared, as if awed. 'You *what?*' Then he grinned. 'God awmighty, you've sure thrown the cat among the pigeons now, Pa.'

By the time the riders drew up before the stoop in a cloud of dust all work around the ranch had ceased. The hands that were on the M-M payroll and had been making ready to ride out to the day's work were now gathered with them, but spread out and watchful.

At the head of the riders Simpson saw a thick-set man with sharp features and a beak nose. Two amber eyes stared out from under dark brows. A Colt nestled on his hip. Gripping the saddle horn and leaning forward Bart Tranter, owner of the Boxed T to the north of the basin, said, 'You got a day to move that wire, McAdam.'

Brad McAdam drew himself up. 'When you finish layin' claim to Ellis Canyon, I'll do that. I've never denied you the water in it.'

'It's free range!' roared Tranter ferociously. 'I'm tryin' to be friendly.'

'I filed on that ten years ago, Tranter,' said Brad McAdam.

'It's on'y your word for that. I've seen no proof.'

'You sayin' my word ain't good enough?' McAdam challenged.

'I'm sayin' I ain't seen proof.'

Brad McAdam glared. 'Then go to the county land office in Serela,' he roared. 'Man, you've been in the basin twelve months. In that time you've made yourself nothin' but a dag-blamed nuisance. This basin was friendly 'til you came. Your ambitions have been ridin' too high a horse lately. I suspect strongly you burnt out Hoss Dakin down on the Boney River, just to buy him out an' acquire his land.'

At that remark Bart Tranter's amber gaze brightened, became hard in its deep-set sockets. He said harshly, though his tone was restrained, 'Still wantin' to be friendly, McAdam, I advise you to pick your words more careful from here on.'

Brad McAdam squared his shoulders, his

gaze sparking like struck flint. 'You do? Well, unfortunately, on certain matters, such as justice, I ain't a prudent man. So I'll also say to you I hear you've been leanin' heavily on widow Mather to get her to sell. Since the unsolved bushwhackin' of her husband, Nathan, that dear woman has had enough to contend with, without you hackin' at her to move out every chance you have.'

Tranter 'humphed', smiled sardonically. 'I figure I'm doin' her a favour. A woman alone in this country ... she don't stand a chance.'

'She'll make out if left alone,' insisted old man McAdam sharply. 'She's lived hereabouts most of her life. The rest of the owners in the basin'll look out for her 'til she can stand on her own. She's a strong woman.'

A sneer curved Tranter's thin lips. 'Well, that's real touchin'. But I heard some ain't so keen on doin' that, heard even, some are eyein' the spread with a view to buy an' wavin' hard money to prove it.'

' "Some" meanin' the Boxed T,' snorted Brad McAdam, contemptuously.

Bart Tranter spread big, bony hands, raised thin, dark eyebrows. 'Meanin' I'm a businessman first, McAdam, as you should be, a sentimentalist last.'

Brad McAdam leaned his spare frame forward aggressively from his position on the stoop. The grey in his eye set hard. He breathed, 'Well, you leave her be, y'hear? I mean that, Tranter.'

A mocking grin spread across the Boxed T owner's lean features. He looked around at the faces of his crew, who were drawn up in a line, with Tranter at their centre. 'You hear that, boys? You hear him threaten me? When all I done was come here peaceable to settle a little disagreement?'

Scoffing titters ran through the hardcases backing Tranter. Some guffawed. Brad McAdam stiffened. Simpson tensed, too— his lawman instincts beginning to sense this could be some sort of set up. Tranter sure had enough gun muscle here to assume that.

Tranter was jeering, 'But I ask you, boys, what has McAdam got to back it up?' He ran his gaze contemptuously over the four M-M hands standing grim-faced in a half circle. Only two wore sidearms. More mocking laughs followed. 'Another thing I heard while ridin' in here,' went on Tranter, 'Abel Cross and two of his hands got bushwhacked on the trail home last night. Real messy job ... so I heard. They say a man named Carl Simpson was bust out of jail, too. It was figured by some in town that he was responsible. He had some kind of run in with Cross ... so I heard.'

A gasp came from Brad McAdam. 'Abe Cross dead?' he said. Taw started forward, too. 'An' that's a damned lie 'bout Carl Simpson!' he breathed, but Carl restrained him with a hand. He said tersely, 'Easy, Taw.' He felt the youth relax, but reluctantly.

The elder McAdam breathed, 'I can't believe it.'

'Yeah, Cross an' two of his hands,' purred Tranter. 'Sad, ain't it? Gettin' to be a man can't ride his own range in peace any more.' Carl became aware now that the Boxed T owner's amber gaze had turned on to himself. For some odd reason he thought it had the glitter of death in it. 'You got a name, mister?' Tranter prompted, though Simpson suspected he already knew it.

He stared, his gaze brittle. 'Don't figure to ride me, Tranter,' he said softly, 'I ain't a widow with a few acres, or a man without a care in the world ridin' home with his hands after a night in town.'

Tranter's lean, sun-burnt features set hard. 'What you tryin' to say, mister?' he breathed. His hand streaked for his sixgun, bolstered high on his hip, but the clicks of Simpson's Colt hammer being drawn full back as it levelled up on the Boxed T owner's midriff ended the play.

A semi-shocked murmur rippled through the assembly—M-M riders and the Boxed T alike. Boxed T riders eased their hands away from gunmetal with studied care. Seemed the opportunity they had maybe been looking for had suddenly taken a bad turn.

Bart Tranter eased his hand away from his sidearm. A deadly grin formed on his narrow features. 'Well, now,' he breathed, 'what have we here? Seems it was true what they said about you in Ladderet. You are *that* Carl Simpson, right? The one that killed the Mosten boys?'

Simpson's stare was cold. Though he hated to use his past reputation he said, 'So you'd best bear it in mind, mister, next time you go for that hogleg.'

The Boxed T owner laughed softly. 'I sure will. But you ain't figurin' on takin' up with McAdam, are you?'

'My business, Tranter,' snapped Carl.

The Boxed T owner chuckled indulgently, looked around him. 'Seems we have a man of few words here, boys,' he crowed. Simpson met Tranter's gaze as it turned back to him. 'Well, I could do with a hot gun like that on *my* payroll,' he said. 'How about it?'

'I'm not for hire.'

Tranter shrugged wide shoulders, pursed thin lips. 'Well, no harm in havin' a little discussion about it, is there?' he said amiably. 'Gettin' to be too many killin's on this range. I'm beginnin' to feel I need some protection.'

Simpson let his eyes range over the hardcases ranked up with Tranter. He doubted if seven he could see had ever seriously ridden a fence line, or branded a steer. He knew a hired gun when he saw one.

'From where I'm standin', seems you have enough already,' he said.

Tranter raised dark brows. 'Always room for improvement, an' the pay's good.'

'You said the law was lookin' for me,' said Simpson.

Tranter raised dark, narrow brows again. 'Yeah. But I don't seriously believe you'd get yourself involved in such wrong doin', bein' such a renowned ex-lawman. I'm sure you'd clear that up quick enough. But I'd be interested to know who pulled those bars for you.'

Simpson suddenly thought he should have kept out of this. However, there were still those traces of the natural lawdog in him that wouldn't allow him to. And instinctively he knew there was something about Tranter—though he'd offered him gunwork—that wasn't friendly towards him. He was beginning to wonder what that something was. And he abruptly felt now he wanted to sting Tranter a little. 'Can't be your confidence that *I* didn't kill Cross stems from the fact that maybe *you* had somethin' to do with it?' he prodded.

Tranter stiffened. All false bonhomie left his features. Dark anger spread across his narrow face. 'By God, mister, what are you drivin' at? No man talks to me like that an' gets away with it. Harkness!'

Off to his left, Simpson caught a slight movement. It was one of Tranter's gunnies, called upon to earn his pay. Simpson's move was swift, the boom of the Colt jarring. A cry came from the hired gun. His Colt dropped from his hand and thudded on to the hard-packed ground, puffing up dust where it hit. Harkness grasped his right shoulder. Blood trickled through his fingers and stained his shirt and vest. He started moaning.

Simpson's Colt hammer clicked again as once more he cocked it and lined it up on Tranter. 'Next man you ask to try a damn-fool trick like that will book *your* ticket to Boot Hill. You understand me, Tranter?'

There was angry movement amongst the Boxed T hardcases; hands clawed close to gunmetal. Tight-lipped and pale Tranter raised his arm. 'Let it lie, boys,' he advised. He swivelled his gaze on to Brad McAdam.

'McAdam. Be warned. Move that wire or it'll get serious between us.'

'If it's true Abe Cross is dead, Tranter,' murmured McAdam, a deathly hint to his tone, 'then it already has, because I strongly suspect you had a hand in it. Get off my land.'

Tranter's grin formed slowly. It resembled the grin of a dominant dog wolf anticipating a victory. He nodded. 'For now, McAdam,' he purred easily. 'For now.'

With a tug at the rein he swung around the big chestnut gelding he was on. 'OK, boys, let's move it. Seems we ain't welcome here right now.'

He grinned again; the same deadly, wolfish grin.

FOUR

As Simpson watched the Boxed T riders head off north cross the grama grass, he slowly holstered his Colt.

'I'm obliged for your assistance,' Brad McAdam said, his long face strained but his grey gaze sincere as he turned it on to Simpson. 'But you've made a bad enemy.'

Simpson nodded, said, 'So have you, I reckon. But both of us, it seems, was given little choice.'

Breaking in Taw blurted urgently, 'Got to git to the Circle C, Pa. I got to be with Lucy, give her my support.'

Old man McAdam nodded, the lines on his face setting even harder. 'I agree.' He rested a large veined hand on Taw's shoulder. 'Maybe this is where you start growin', boy. But watch the trail. Tranter's made his intentions clear. Like Mr Simpson has already suggested, I'd lay a thousand dollars it was Tranter's gunnies that laid Abe and his boys low. It's now clear that man's ruthless ambition has no bounds.'

Taw was wide-eyed. 'You really think it *was* Tranter?'

'Who else could it be?' snorted the older McAdam.

Simpson cleared his throat, butted in. 'The trick is, Mr McAdam, a man has to prove his suspicions and allegations. When I suggested it, I was just fishin'. My gut tells me I'm right, but that ain't proof.'

McAdam growled. 'Damn it, don't I know? Ain't John Patter been rammin' that same fact down my throat every time I bring up Tranter's shenanigans?'

'The marshal of Hell?' said Simpson.

McAdam nodded again. 'But he can't do much, I guess. His power don't go beyond the town limits. However, I don't think that would stop him if he feels strong enough 'bout somethin'. Like Abe Cross's killin', for instance.'

'He gave me that impression,' said Simpson.

'John believes in upholdin' the law,' assured McAdam.

'Maybe he should approach the county or federal authorities,' suggested Simpson.

'There's Sheriff Tom Boot in Serela,' said McAdam. 'That's the county seat. Guess he'll have to step in, though he's spread thin. On'y got two deputies. Guess we are expected to look after our own trouble down here most of the time.' The M-M owner's grey gaze lifted hopefully and studied Simpson's battered features. 'Reckon you wouldn't consider stayin' on awhile?'

Simpson found emotions beginning to tug at him, the urge to right a wrong done. It had always been so strong. But damn it, he was heading for California. However, much as it annoyed him, something inside him was now urging him to do otherwise.

He'd heard that three men had been bushwhacked and that he had been made a suspect. He had heard that another man had been murdered, his widow left to fend almost for herself. He'd seen Tranter in action. Clearly the man believed a mess of gun hands would give him power and he was prepared to use that power to further his apparently insatiable need for range and to hell with what that entailed. This was clearly lawless land he'd ridden into, the county law distant and apparently impoverished. But he was sick of fighting other men's battles. No, damn it, he was heading for California.

'Guess not, McAdam,' he declined.

Brad McAdam tightened his lips, looked disappointed but nodded. 'Understood,' he said. 'Ma'll fix you up with vittles. Again, safe journey, Simpson.' He turned to the hands around him. 'OK, boys. Show's over. We got work to do. But watch yourselves from here on. Tranter's made his intentions clear.' Then he turned to

Taw. 'Git on over to the Circle C, son. See what comfort and support you can give. Let Anson know our feelin's on it. Bein' Abe's eldest boy, guess he'll be takin' up the reins, though his mother Eileen's a strong woman an' there could be a dispute about that. Tell them the M-M'll support any move they wish to make in this, providin' it's sensible.'

Taw hitched his gunbelt, looked satisfied. 'Will do.' Simpson met the young Mc-Adam's stare as he turned to him. 'Sorry you ain't joinin' us, Carl,' Taw said. 'Real sorry. Frankly, I can't understand why not, way you took on Tranter.'

Simpson shrugged. 'Maybe some day you will, Taw.'

The younger McAdam nodded, then shrugged. 'Maybe.' He stuck out a hand. 'S'long. Though painful, been a real treat knowin' you.'

Simpson smiled, took the hand. 'An' you, Taw. Take care now.'

Within moments Simpson found himself

alone on the stoop. M   watched the hands and b   ride off on to the range, two pa   going in a different direction. I   all framed in the golden rays of th   morning sun, that yellowed the dust they disturbed. Then he watched Taw head off fast towards the sunrise. He sighed. For some reason he felt guilty about not taking up McAdam's offer, but he soon shook the feeling off. He had no reason to feel that way. Damn it, he owed this basin nothing, unlike Ladderet where he had grown up and where the woman he had hoped to marry had been gunned down by the vicious Mosten boys.

As the memory of it came back, pain stabbed at him. He remembered his bride to be, Janet, as she came running out of the house to meet him, alive, vibrant, happy. He had been invited to supper. He remembered the buzz of the big calibre slug that had been meant for him but had torn into her instead; remembered the

It had fountained out of the big blood vessel in her throat as it was rent apart. She had died almost instantly in his arms, her gore still splashing on to him.

With the memory still nauseatingly real to him he grabbed the awning post nearby, one of several supporting the stoop. He squeezed hard; squeezed to try and erase the terrible pain the recollection still engendered after three long years. Not only that, there had been the boy's death as well ...

'Mr Simpson?'

He turned to see Flora McAdam smiling at him. Then he saw her recoil, uncertainty come to her features, perhaps a little anxiety. Then she said, 'There is death in your eyes. I'm sorry. Perhaps I disturbed you, picked the wrong time.'

Simpson wiped the recollections away. But he knew they would be back when something else cropped up to resurrect them.

'No, ma'am,' he said quickly. 'Just that

sometimes a man gets to recallin' things he shouldn't. He should learn to bury the past.'

Flora McAdam's strong face softened to mellow lines. 'Not all of the past, Mr Simpson. All of life, the good and the bad, should be remembered. The trick is to come to terms with it.'

Simpson stared at her, admiring her wisdom. 'Ma'am, I never thought of it like that. It sure puts things into perspective.'

He thought he saw a hint of colour touch the white of her throat. As if slightly embarrassed she fussed with her apron. 'I just came to say I have your food ready when you want to pick it up. It should see you on to the next town. If you're heading for California still, that will be Grand Creek, one hundred miles west of here, other side of the Pecon Hills.'

'I feel I should pay you something,' he said.

'Brad said "No",' she demurred. 'I'll say it, too. I'll hand your vittles to you when you've saddled your horse and are ready to leave. But a word of warning if I may, Mr Simpson: your trail will take you across the southern end of Bart Tranter's range. He has men everywhere. You'll now be on his list.'

She turned and went back into the house. Simpson watched her go. That was one smart lady, he thought. 'I'll heed that,' he promised, before he turned to go and saddle the big roan.

FIVE

At the head of his men Bart Tranter rode hard across the grama grass, away from the M-M ranch. Anger seethed within him. No man made a fool of Bart Tranter. No man. But Simpson had. And he would pay, pay hard for that *and* other things. It was that sonofabitch who had shot down his cousins in Ladderet, the Mostens. Though Simpson hadn't known it, brooded Tranter, for a year he had trailed him, vengeance etched in him until the trail had gone cold and he had. Then he had met up with Coley Das once more, who, over drinks, had outlined his plan to rob the Miler City bank. Das had said he was short of a partner he could trust, and, he had added happily, fate had provided himself, Bart Tranter. Long back now they'd soldiered together—Tranter smirked as he remembered—if you can call being in Bloody Bill Anderson's set-up soldiering.

The job, he recalled, had gone as smooth as silk. With his split from the robbery safe in his saddlebags, he had laid low. It had been the one chance he had been looking for—to rake together some real money. He wasn't going to louse it up by doing something stupid, like Coley Das did. After the heist Das had boozed, boasted and spent his way across most of Kansas. They'd finally caught up with him and hanged him in Miler City as part of the Fourth of July celebrations. Tranter thought happily, he had gone down like a man, had Coley. They had been unable to extract from him who had partnered him in the robbery, even though they'd beat the shit out of him.

Tranter had waited a further year. Then he had moved south and bought the Boxed T. Now, by some extraordinary twist of fortune, the man he had hunted for a long year, Simpson, had been delivered straight into his hands. Though he was mad things hadn't gone as planned at the M-M that morning, he felt grim joy that Simpson had been dropped right into his lap. And if Simpson had agreed to take the job he had offered him, he would have had the bastard right where he could be dealt with—and pick his own time and his own place to do it. And at last McAdam had risen to the bait he'd been annoying him with recently. Tranter chuckled. The old fool had finally laid on an excuse for him to get at him, wiring off the water in Ellis Canyon like he had. He stared at the ground passing beneath the gelding's belly, grim joy warming him. Despite the way things had gone at the M-M just now, whoever watched over him had sure done a job for him this time, he decided.

So as soon as he was into the mesas that separated the M-M and the Boxed T ranges he drew rein on his big mount and turned in the saddle. Now, though, the elation he had experienced at finding Simpson had long since gone and he settled his cold glare on the mean-faced rider nearest to him. 'Collins, I want that damned Simpson taken out,' he rasped harshly. 'Right now.' Then he swung his gaze on to the wounded gunny, Cole Harkness. The shootist was groggy and clearly shocked, but Tranter felt no sympathy. 'How bad is it?' he snapped.

'Hurtin' like hell, Mr Tranter,' Harkness gritted. 'That sonofabitch ...' He gasped, keeled out of the saddle in a dead faint and hit the ground hard. The front of his shirt was covered with blood.

With eyes as hard as amber, Tranter stared down at Harkness. Some damned top gun he turned out to be! He swung round, gazed at a fat, surly-looking hardcase nearby, atop a rangy piebald. 'Well, get him into Hell, Ambrose,' he ordered with resignation. 'See Doc Crowley. Tell him to patch him up best he can. Then see John Patter. Report

Harkness's wounding to him; tell him that it was Simpson who done it. Also tell him McAdam's been sheltering him. You got that?'

Macy Ambrose nodded. 'Sure, Mr Tranter,' he said and climbed down to attend to Harkness.

Tranter swung his gaze immediately to the other man he had singled out earlier, Montana Collins. 'You hear me, Montana? You say you're the best rifleman I got. Now's your chance to prove it. I want you to get Simpson good an' I don't care how you do it. An' I want no slip up this time. There's been one too many already.'

Tall, stringy, fox-faced Montana Collins nodded, massaged the white, vivid knife scar down his left cheek. 'He'll get his, Mr Tranter, you bet,' he said and pulled the grey he was riding around and rode off, back towards the M-M spread. Tranter reckoned Collins was a patient man. He would wait, watch the M-M. When Simpson showed he would pick his spot and make his strike.

Meanwhile, calming now he was getting things going his way again, Tranter turned to his men. 'OK, boys. Back to the ranch.' He forced a grim smile. 'Still work to be done, like tearing down McAdam's wire, for right now he's just used up his chances of me bein' nice about it.'

Tobacco-stained smiles stretched across hardcase faces greeted his words. 'I got another little surprise for McAdam, too,' Tranter added happily, 'like I'm goin' to blow that narrow in the canyon and block him off from that precious water he's bein' so close about.'

Delighted guffaws greeted his words this time. One said, 'Boss, when you start movin', you move fast. I like that.'

Tranter grinned some more. 'Come to think of it, so do I, Jake. So do I,' he repeated and kneed his big horse into motion. He even began to whistle a jaunty tune.

As Tranter sat outlining his schemes to his men, Simpson was climbing up on to his big roan's back at the McAdam ranch-house. Atop of it he nudged it into a trot west, towards the serrated purple line of the Peton Hills and away from the sprawl of M-M buildings. Mrs McAdam had been there to hand him his victuals and bid him goodbye. He had offered to stay until the hands returned, but she had waved his suggestion aside, saying there were still two men around the place to look out for her.

With that reassurance he urged the horse into a steady lope, out across the grama grass. After half an hour of easy riding under the building heat of the mid-morning sun he thought he detected movement, high on the ridge that led away towards the hills from the red mesas to the north. But the distance was about a mile and he figured it could have been just a play of the light, or wind-stirred brush, or even a steer. But there was no breeze to speak of, and, as far as he could see, no cattle up there. Then he saw a momentary flash of sunlight on metal, or glass. He rubbed his bruised chin. Well, man, that told another story and one he should heed.

He set his jaw into a firm line. With the sighting he could feel his nerve ends were already keening up to a high pitch of alertness. It could be nothing—a carelessly discarded bottle by some cowhand at one time, he had to admit, but then, it could be a hell of a lot more. He'd sure stirred things up with Bart Tranter. And the boss of the Boxed T had come over as a vindictive type of man who would let nothing pass.

Simpson rode on, but loosened both his Colt and his Winchester, which was in the saddle boot at his right knee. Then he set his hat so that his eyes would be in the shade of the wide brim. His grey gaze peered out, scanning the terrain ahead with thorough, probing sweeps.

Four more miles of steady riding took him into the foothills of the Pecons. High, riven hills swelling away like choppy waves to craggy, even more rough country in the blue haze ahead. He had seen nothing more since that first movement and the reflected light beaming out at him for a moment. Though it was reassuring he hadn't, he didn't slacken his vigilance. He had learnt long ago not to do that.

The rocky draw he entered a quarter of an hour later set him right on edge. It was made for ambush and the start of two magpies out of brush a hundred yards up the trail rasping their harsh noise had him throwing the reins over the horse's head and moving fast. He rolled low off the roan, while reaching for his Winchester, dragging it out of its scabbard as he went to ground. There he scrambled for cover.

The immediate flat crack of a rifle and the snarl of lead off rocks nearby sent Simpson pounding the rocky ground deeper into the crags, but happy his instincts had paid off and he was making the bushwhacking bastard up there earn his pay. Now more lead raged about him, but Simpson had the gut feeling the man was already guessing.

And he was bone certain of another thing: he had to get above his attacker. He snaked through the brush heading upwards, anxiously throwing a stare towards the place from where the gunshots had come. He saw nothing he could hit, just powder smoke. A quick glance behind him told him his big roan was still standing on the trail, where he had left it groundhitched by the reins he had dropped over its head.

The ambush rifle snapped flat noise again and Simpson's gut snarled up with anguish when he saw his horse drop down on to its belly, its legs splayed out Then its head hit the ground with a bony thud. Simpson could see its eyes were rolling and blinking. Then its pink tongue lolled out into the dust from death-slackened jaws and two puffs of dust rose as it exhaled its last breath. Appalled, Simpson now saw blood was seeping from a neat hole, centre of its forehead. More blood spilled briefly from the beast's mouth, but it didn't move again, except to give off a long quiver that vibrated its limbs throughout its body before it became still.

Instant wrath surged up into Simpson's craw along with a sense of deep loss which near overwhelmed him for a second or two. Over the years he and that roan had ridden many long trails together. He'd become deeply attached to it. Grim-faced, he clamped his hand hard around his Winchester and started up the slope again. He had one thing in mind. That low-down ...

As he made his run he heard the beat of hooves, hammering up the draw. Simpson saw the ambusher break cover two hundred yards ahead of him. Driven by rage and the need to do damage Simpson raised his rifle. It was a long shot, the target moving fast, but he had to try it.

As he pressed the trigger the Winchester kicked back hard into his shoulder. He saw dust powder off the rocks close behind the rider. But by the time he had jacked in another load, the bushwhacker had moved behind a screen of boulders.

Now Simpson found his mind buzzing with questions. Why had the sonofabitch gone off the trail, instead of sticking to it? If he had figured he'd failed in his bushwhack attempt and was intent on running, that was what he should have done. Reason said so. But, Simpson soon realized, that no-good bastard was heading for the same high ground he was making for. He narrowed his eyelids. He decided it would remain a mystery why the scum hadn't done that self same thing in the first place.

Anxious, Simpson began to move rapidly. As he did the snarl of the ambush rifle started up again. The plume of grey-blue gunsmoke he saw snaking in the breeze on the ridge top now confirmed his suspicions and the fact that he had been beaten to the high ground.

Lead raged off the rock two inches from Simpson's head. Slivers of stone drew blood from his right cheek.

Simpson went to ground again and began snaking through the rock and brush, ignoring the spears of pain the rough ground caused to his savagely bruised body. This time, however, he knew he would be exposed as soon as he had to cross open ground. And twenty yards ahead he could see that that was all there was.

Grim-faced and cut to the heart by having to witness the death of his horse, Simpson pressed close to the ground, the need for vengeance rising rampant. It also induced a certain recklessness. Somehow, he had to get that bastard up there to show himself.

He reared and hammered four shots at the ridge top, powdering dust and dirt into the stark blue sky, then rolled, crashing through the clawing brush while heading for a huge boulder that stuck out like a rotten tooth up the bank side. He deliberately made noise.

The rifle snarled again. Lead lashed through the wiry branches around Simpson. Now slugs 'whanged' off the rock he was scrambling behind.

Simpson went round the boulder fast. On its far side he pulled his rifle into his left shoulder so he exposed as little as possible of himself and to maybe fool that bastard up there a little by popping up on the wrong side. He had learned long ago to use the long gun on any shoulder he put it to, though he was most accurate from the right.

Now he could see the ambusher's head and shoulders exposed, his clearly anxious gaze searching for him, his long gun drawn up and sighted, ready to shoot in an instant. And when Simpson showed himself, he watched the bushwhacker turn anxiously and rapidly towards him, but

Simpson knew the sonofabitch had lost the edge he needed. He squeezed off. He heard the man yell, saw his rifle drop as he clutched his left side before he ducked out of sight.

Elated, Simpson uncoiled himself and began pounding up the steep rock-strewn side of the draw, cursing the unsuitability of his high-heeled riding boots for such activity.

Before he reached the top of the gully he heard the pound of hooves, but he didn't fully abandon caution. He skirted the rough ground below the rimrock, using the ledge of an overhang to cover him.

He popped up way to the left of where he had hit the bushwhacker, rifle levelled, trigger squeezed up to the limit before detonation. But he discovered the bird had flown. Already Simpson could see dust rising above the cluster of rocks maybe a quarter of a mile away.

'Damnation!' he roared and threw down his hat.

Ten minutes later, and for the second time in two days, he found himself hoisting his saddle and possibles ready for a hike, but it was back to the M-M spread this time.

His heart was heavy. He was now fully mourning the loss of the roan. But the sound of many hooves approaching, pounding the rocky ground ahead, quickly cleared the sense of loss from his mind and sent it concentrating on the business to hand. He dropped the saddle and lifted his Winchester. There was no time to seek cover.

It came as a full surprise when the posse of twelve men clattered into the draw and reined up before him. Simpson could see John Patter, the marshal of Hell, was at its head. Simpson also saw eleven rifles lift and line up on him, hard-eyed riders behind them. They looked loaded for bear.

When he was close Patter waved his sixgun, said easily, almost conversationally, 'Heard shootin'.'

Simpson nodded, his gut taut. 'You did.' Then he gazed at the mean-looking posse. 'But getting straight to it—in case you're figurin' I killed Abel Cross and his men—you're wrong all the way down the line, Patter, y'hear?' he rasped out.

'That's exactly what we're figurin' you did, mister,' snarled one of the riders, a young man in his early twenties, 'an' we got a rope here to see that justice is done, pronto.'

John Patter leaned forward in his saddle and stared at the rider who had just spoken. 'I know you got good cause—but ease it, Clute,' he said. Then he turned his grey stare. Simpson met it defiantly. Patter said, 'How come you know about Abel Cross, if you didn't do it?'

Simpson began to tell him and watched as Patter's face grew redder. 'God damn,' he burst out interrupting. 'Taw broke you out?' Then stopped, as if to gather himself. 'Well, we followed the double tracks from the jailhouse to the M-M, followed the single track into these here hills. Your roan leaves a definite trail.' Patter glowered now. 'An' you're sayin' that young whipper-snapper pulled out my jail bars?' He snorted. 'Why, God damn him for his impudence. An' you say Bart Tranter was at the M-M this morning? What was the reason?'

Again, Simpson told him.

'Brad's strung wire across Ellis Canyon?' blurted Patter. 'If that ain't the most damn fool thing for a man to do, things the way they are right now. It's just what that sonofabitch Tranter wanted Brad to do.'

Simpson said, 'McAdam figured it was the right thing to do. He said he was sick to death of Tranter layin' claim to it. He said when Tranter quit doin' that, he'd open it up again so's the Boxed T could water their cattle there as usual.'

'Whut happened then?' pursued Patter. His chubby, but tired-looking face had become even more grim. The posse leaned forward intently, too.

'Tranter turned nasty, went for his gun,' said Simpson. 'I persuaded him it wasn't a good idea, but it was plain to me he'd come to make gun trouble and called on a shootist named Harkness to start things rollin'. Well, I had no recourse but to shoot and wound him.'

Patter's grey gaze narrowed. '*You* threw down on Cole Harkness?'

Simpson glowered up at the marshal. 'More like he threw down on me. I wasn't about to let him blow me away. Hell, I'm tryin' to ride out of this damned basin,' he added bitterly. 'But all I seem to get is damned wet-eared kids puttin' me afoot in the desert, saddlemen advisin' me to walk—though God rest their souls, now, I guess—an' a bushwhacker tryin' to kill me just now.' He continued to glare wrathfully at Patter and pointed. 'Look what that sonofabitch done to my horse.'

Patter spread his lips thinly as he stared down at the dead roan. 'Well, that's too bad about the horse. It was a fine animal.'

Again his narrow gaze came up. 'But, mister, you seem to draw trouble like meat draws flies.'

Simpson growled angrily, 'None of my wantin', I can tell you. Now what I want to know is what's the law around here goin' to do about it? If this ain't Bart Tranter's doin'—settin' up this ambush—I'll eat my hat.'

With that Patter straightened from his slump in the saddle, clearly alarmed. 'Now hold on, mister. You can't go around accusin' people off the top of your head like that. Despite bein' a damned nuisance, Tranter has standin' in this area.'

'McAdam seems to think he's the one causin' all the trouble you seem to have,' said Simpson. 'How about that?'

Tranter tugged at the brim of his cream stetson, as if expressing his irritation and disquiet. 'Brad McAdam can be less than prudent with his opinions sometimes,' he snorted. 'Figure his idea to wire off the water in Ellis Canyon ain't one of his brighter notions. Damn, that would be like wavin' a red rag at a bull where Bart Tranter is concerned. An' if you took McAdam's side, you straightaway bought yourself in, so don't go on about it if Tranter figured on sendin' one of his gunnies to take a pot-shot at you, seein' as you've already disabled one of his top men.'

Angered by that, Simpson roared, 'I wasn't takin' up with anybody! I was savin' my own hide. An' I'm tryin' to get out of this damned basin! From the word go I've wanted no part of this country. But now that bushwhackin' sonofabitch—whoever he was—has shot down my horse, things have changed mightily. Now I got a side of my own to consider. Nothin' to do with the M-M, or McAdam. You'd better understand I thought a heap of that horse.'

Patter moved irritably in the saddle. He snorted indignantly, 'Well, don't shout at me, mister. An' there's still the matter of

Abel Cross's shootin'—an' the killin' of his two hands, Jimmy Sands an' Lew Beel.'

'Well, don't come lookin' in this direction,' Simpson said emphatically. 'I was headin' for the M-M with Taw McAdam when that happened.' He leaned forward, stared keenly. 'But just ask yourself one question about that business, Patter. How come Tranter knew so much about it when he visited the M-M early this mornin'?'

Marshal Patter wiped his dark, silky moustache with a long index finger. He glared from under dark, bushy brows. 'What you tryin' to say, mister?'

'I've heard other men on this range have been gunned down an' Tranter's been the only one to benefit from it,' hinted Simpson.

Patter rocked uncomfortably in his saddle. 'Bin nothin' at all that could allow a man to point a finger at Tranter,' he grunted. 'He's just a rock-hard businessman who don't let sentiment cloud his judgement.'

Simpson glared. 'Well, I heard those words somewhere else today,' he growled, 'from Tranter. So answer me this: why is his outfit so top heavy with gun-slicks if he ain't lookin' for trouble?'

Patter spat, glared. 'Who's sayin' it is?'

Simpson stared up at the sombre-faced lawman. 'Damn it,' he snorted. 'He was bristlin' with them this mornin'. If I've learnt one thing in my life, it's how to pick out a gun sharp when I see one.'

'Big damned Carl Simpson, hero of Ladderet,' sneered one of the possemen. 'Come to save *us*, now?'

Simpson glared, his cold anger flaring. 'I've come to save nobody, mister,' he breathed. 'But I've just had my hoss killed, a gentle animal I valued highly. Now, by God, I want my pound of flesh.'

Restlessly, Patter tugged at his moustache once more. 'Well, hell, this is gettin' us nowhere,' he growled. He scowled at the nearest man. 'Lucas, take Simpson's saddle and bags.' Now Carl met the marshal's gaze as it turned back to him. 'Climb up behind me if you want a lift to the M-M. Seems that's where your friends are in this valley. An' seems that's where you can prove your claim.'

'What about that damned bushwhacker?' snorted Simpson. 'I put lead in him. Could be he ain't got very far.'

Now Patter gnawed at his moustache. It seemed a habit he had formed when he was having to think hard on something.

'How long ago since he took off?' he said after moments.

'Quarter of an hour.'

Patter sucked more on his moustache, then said, 'Bad country out there. Not ideal for trackin' a man.' He paused and nodded vigorously. 'Though we got men as can do it. We found you.'

'So the sonofabitch goes free, huh?' snorted Simpson.

He watched Patter become a little disgruntled at being addressed so forthrightly. The marshal turned to his posse.

Simpson could see they were mostly townspeople—except the one Patter had named Clute, who looked a saddleman and a tall, scarred, mean-faced individual he didn't know the name of yet. Certainly, most looked to be more used to counter trading and other urban activities than seeking out a trail. 'Well, what do you think, boys?' Patter said.

'We came after Simpson,' snorted one. He motioned towards the tall, dark-eyed, mean-looking posseman. 'An', thanks to Hewson here, we've found him. You seem to figure he's clean. But we've on'y his word he's been bushwhacked ...'

'You think I'd shoot my own damn horse?' interrupted Simpson. 'What for? Like I keep sayin' I want out of this valley, but now that won't be before I know why I've been shot at an' why my horse was killed.'

The young saddleman named Clute leaned forward. 'Well, strange as it may be, I'm with you, mister,' he said. 'There's a rotten smell to the whole of this business. An' we can soon find out from Taw if you've been tellin' us the truth.'

'Well, thank you for that, boy,' growled Simpson. He glowered at Patter. 'So, you backin' this man, Marshal? Seems he's the on'y one showin' any sense here.'

Patter reddened, puffed his cheeks out. 'Mister, don't come all abrasive on me. I ain't had a chance to offer my own opinion yet. But now I have, I, too, reckon we should go after that sonofabitch. An' now I'm sayin' we are. By the way, that boy you're ratin' is Clute Cross, Abel's youngest.'

Simpson switched and narrowed his gaze, nodded—could see the resemblance. Short, stocky, keen-eyed, like he remembered Cross had been. 'Seems your pa raised you good,' he said. Then he glared at Patter. 'So are we goin' now? Time's awastin'.'

'Who in the hell do you think you are, mister?' snorted a posseman. 'We all have businesses to run. We ain't doin' it while on a wild goose chase. We came after you, is all.'

The mean-eyed one named Hewson spat tobacco juice. 'Well, I'm for goin' on,' he growled.

Clute Cross gazed at the protesting posseman with steady grey eyes. 'Quit if you want to, Saul,' he said. 'But be sure I'm goin' on, too, like Hewson. We'll maybe learn somethin'.'

Saul Pollard, of Pollard's Emporium, growled, looked resentful. 'Now, you ain't no right to talk like that, Clute. I ain't no quitter. I want the killers of your father, Lew an' Jimmy brought to justice just as keen as you do.'

'Then maybe the answers to that are up the trail, like Clute hinted,' interjected Simpson. 'I know I put lead in him. But while we're arguin' the issue, he's puttin' ground between us.'

John Patter nodded sombrely. 'I'm comin' round to agreein'.' He stared around. 'So those wantin' to come, fall in. Those that don't can git ... You climbin' up, Simpson?'

Carl swung up behind the stocky marshal. Straightaway, the lawman urged the big roan he was riding on.

Surprising Simpson, the whole of the posse fell in behind, but some had sullen looks and cursed roundly at the inconvenience of it all. However, Simpson had a sneaking feeling they wouldn't quit, but that they had to gripe about it all the same.

SIX

Taw McAdam skirted the town of Hell, quirting his bay hard. Heading east, the trail to Circle C boiled with his dust. The ranch lay across the basin from the M-M, the arid badlands he had led Abel and his boys into—only yesterday?—shimmering far to the south-west.

Taw's heart was heavy. It had seemed a hell of a joke at the time, leading Abel and his boys into the badlands then back into town, but now, with his own best horse dead and maybe Abel, Lew and Jimmy dead as well because he had, it was not so funny. Pa was right. He had a lot of growing up to do, and it had started right now.

It was past noon when he pounded into the Circle C ranch confines. A low wall surrounded it and, like the M-M, the windows in the ranch-house were small, with rifle slits cut in the stout shutters. Remnants from a past that had called upon the Cross family to stand off Indian raids more than once. Barns, bunkhouse and corrals were spread around it.

He dropped off the lathered bay and began walking it around to cool it. Lucy was already on the stoop and now came running towards him. She flung herself into his arms. 'Oh, Taw. I prayed that you'd come.' She seemed not to notice his battered face.

'Easy, honey,' he said. He kissed the blonde curls on top of her head, which was now pressed to his chest. He could smell the faint hint of lavender.

Almost immediately someone bawled, 'Lucy! Come away from him. You know Pa's feelin's regardin' Taw.'

The young McAdam looked up to see the tall, lean figure of Anson Cross, Abel's eldest, coming at a run from the corral by the river. He was carrying a rifle.

Lucy lifted her head off Taw's chest. She stared at her brother. 'Pa's dead, Anson,' she sobbed bitterly. 'Ain't that enough for now?'

Anson's reply was harsh as he drew close. 'Mebbe if Taw hadn't come sparkin' an' foolin' around t'other night, Pa would have been alive now. You thought o' that?'

Taw felt a coolness grip his stomach at the words, for he knew all too well they could be true. But Lucy shrilled, 'That's unfair. You've no right to talk like that.'

'I got every damned right,' snarled Anson.

Several riders were coming in from the range. Taw knew the Circle C ran eight regular riders during spring roundup. Seemed most were staying close to home today.

He gazed at Anson. 'I came to offer the condolences of the M-M,' he said evenly. 'Pa said he was prepared to side you all the way on this. So am I.'

At that Anson seemed to relent a little. 'Well, I thank you fer that. But it still don't alter other matters. Pa's wishes will still be respected.'

'Anson! Enough of that.'

The sharp command came from behind Taw. He turned to see Eileen Cross, Abel's second wife, on the stoop—a tall, big-boned, severe-looking woman. Her hands were akimbo. Looking at her height, Taw had always reckoned there was no mistaking who Anson took after, for Abel had been a short, stocky person. Lucy had always favoured Abel's side—apple-shaped, though trim with it.

'Your father is dead and things have changed,' Mrs Cross was saying. She motioned to one of the hands nearby. 'Rains, take Taw's horse and cool it down, groom it, then feed it. Come on into the house, Taw. I can only apologize for my son's bad manners.'

'Ma!' Anson strode towards the stoop

and stared at her. There was a hint of warning in his voice. 'This ain't right. You know how Pa felt.'

Taw hesitated at the stoop steps. 'Mebbe I should go, ma'am,' he said uneasily. 'I don't want to cause family trouble, particularly at a time like this. I just felt I had to come to Lucy, see what comfort I could give and offer the help of the M-M to find the sonsofbitches that did it.'

Eileen Cross nodded, her head held high. She was clearly bearing her grief with dignity. 'I know that, Taw. And it is most welcome. We do the buryin' at sundown and I wish you to attend.' Her grey stare fastened on Anson. 'You hear that, son?'

Taw saw Anson's lips tighten, but he said nothing.

When he didn't Taw offered, thinking he should say it, 'I'm sure Pa would have been here, too, but there has been trouble with the Boxed T. He wants to stay close.'

Immediately, Anson turned, his grey

look narrow and keen. 'Tranter?' he said. 'Damn him. What's he up to now?'

Taw explained what had happened at the M-M that morning.

'An' this Carl Simpson backed you?' Anson growled, his gaze rounding with disbelief. 'Why, he's the one suspected of killin' Pa, Jimmy Sands and Lew Beel. Clute's with the posse that lit out after him.'

Taw knew Clute Cross was Abel's youngest son. He said, 'Well, I'll tell you now, Anson, your pa's death was nothin' to do with Carl Simpson. He was with me the whole night. I broke him out of jail.'

'You what!' Anson stared. 'God damn it, Ma. You listenin'? An' why ain't *we* ridin'?'

The words didn't seem to affect Eileen Cross all that much. She said, 'I'm listenin'. An' why we ain't ridin'—as you well know—Marshal Patter advised against it, said some men, heated and angry being close, might live to regret their actions when they caught up with Simpson and he didn't want to head a lynching party. So go on with your story, Taw.'

Taw decided to come clean, explained again what had happened between him and Simpson and how he got the bruises. He also told of Carl's role as lawman of Ladderet in the Con Valley war. Then went on, 'Fact is, talkin' as a former lawman, Simpson reckoned that mebbe Tranter was in on your pa's killin'. Been thinkin' about that myself on the way over here. Tranter sure got to know about it damned quick to roll up at the M-M at dawn this mornin' an' tell us about it. An' that man is land-hungry enough to do anythin', I figure.'

Though Anson Cross looked to be thinking hard, he finally shook his head, rubbed his square, dimpled chin. 'That can't be a reason,' he said. 'It don't make sense. Damn it, comin' right down to it, it *could* have been you an' this here Simpson!'

'Anson!' Eileen Cross's outraged call lashed out from the stoop. 'That's enough. We all know Taw better than that.'

'Pa couldn't stand him,' countered Anson bitterly. 'So do we know him? Like Pa used to say, Taw's reputation in this basin ain't ever been held up as a shinin' example.'

Eileen Cross snorted, 'You also know very well your Pa never got over what happened to his first-born, Clarissa—your stepsister. She reminded him so much of his first wife after she died of the cholera, it clouded his thinking on suitors ever after.'

Anson stiffened for moments—Taw sensed this might be the start of the tussle as to who was to wear the trousers at the Circle C in future—before Anson seemed to grudgingly relax. 'Well, I guess so,' he rumbled. He made a conciliatory gesture. 'Must say I've allus found Taw regular enough. Allus glad Pa never caught up with him. An' I reckon Pa never tried all that hard, either, truth be known.'

'So let us have an end to it,' ordered Mrs Cross. 'Now come into the house, Taw. Have you eaten?'

'I had breakfast.'

'Then bein' after noon you ain't eaten.'

When Taw pushed his empty plate away he gazed across the common room at Lucy and Mrs Cross, who were now sitting on a cowhide settee near the west window, across from him. They were sewing. Taw heard that that was how some women coped with their grief, by doing something all the time. Lucy, though, all the time he had eaten had hardly taken her blue, round, unhappy gaze off him. But both women were quiet. Taw had a hunch they were actually grieving hard, sitting stiff and pale like they were, though they were trying their best to hide it.

'Mrs Cross,' he said, finding it difficult to come up with the right words, guessing by the recent tension outside that that was maybe the start of who was to head the Circle C in future, 'has Anson expressed what he intends to do now your husband's dead? He bein' the eldest an' all.'

Eileen Cross's gaze stayed on her sewing. 'As has been explained, Marshal Patter advised us to leave the matter of the shooting with him and stay close to home, so that was decided for Anson, on my insistence,' she said. Though the words came out gentle, there was force behind them. 'But Clute felt the family should be represented and it was finally agreed he rode with the posse.' Her gaze came up from her work momentarily. There was pride in it. 'For his age, unlike Anson who can be hot-headed, Clute has a very level head. And if what you say is true about this Carl Simpson, it makes me hope the rest of the posse don't do anything foolish when they catch up with him, hope that Marshal Patter is able to deal with it.' Then she sighed. 'I sometimes find men are all too ready with the rope in matters of this sort.'

That out Taw immediately realized that the possibility of a lynching hadn't occurred to him and he felt, besides guilt, real concern for his new-found friend. Indeed, a rope was all too readily used in this country as a quick judge and jury. 'Well, I can only say amen to that, ma'am, havin' made a friend of the man, an' all,' he said.

He found his thoughts now wondering exactly what *had* happened to Carl, whether, even, he was still alive. Though he wanted to remain with Lucy, he reckoned, as soon as the burying of Abel Cross was done, he should be heading back to the M-M, for Pa had his troubles, too, and so, maybe, had Carl.

He explained his decision to Lucy. She looked unhappy, but agreed after Eileen Cross's brusque prompting, saying that a man had to do what he thought was best and the woman should support him. Taw had doubts if that would apply to the future running of the Circle C, though. But he was glad to have such a strong-minded ally at this time with regard to Lucy.

When Taw rode away from the Circle C, the sun was sinking behind the low blue line of the Pecon Hills, the sky layers of red, gold and purple cloud above and around the red orb. Dark began settling over the basin.

Maybe a hundred people had ridden in from Hell and small ranches around to be at the burial of Abel Cross. Grant Perkins, the town's blacksmith and acting preacher, had spoken kind words over the grave while Lucy had sobbed beside her brother and mother. God damn it, thought Taw unhappily as he urged the bay on, he was now torn real hard about the decision to leave Lucy, but knew it had to be.

SEVEN

Up on the horse's rump behind Marshal John Patter, Simpson had already discovered it to be a real uncomfortable experience. The trail they followed was plain enough, though, and they immediately found traces of blood, making it clear the bushwhacker was wounded. He was not moving fast, maybe anticipating no chase after shooting Simpson's mount.

Soon the trail led them on to the long ridge that took them out of the Pecons as it melded in with the mesas and canyons.

Speaking over his shoulder Patter warned, waving a hand, 'Through them lies the Boxed T.'

'Well, hell, that sure says somethin' to me,' Simpson grunted. He took a needed drink from his canteen.

'Me too, mebbe,' said Patter. He spat cotton and momentarily glared at the grilling sun.

Coming off the ridge, the trail they followed went into a line of fir and aspen sprawling alongside a stream that gurgled out of the massive canyon ahead. Then they saw the big grey horse standing cropping grass a hundred and fifty or so yards on. They could see no rider and in front of him, Simpson felt Patter tense. The marshal turned. 'Find cover,' he ordered the posse, and swung his big roan into the shade of the trees.

When the posse were dismounted Patter said while mopping his brow, 'What do you think, Simpson?'

Carl shrugged. 'Mebbe he fell off an' he's dead up there. Mebbe I hit him worse than I thought.' He gripped his rifle. 'I reckon I'll go take a look see.'

From close by Clute Cross, young, lean and sunburned, muttered, 'I'm comin' with you.'

Simpson stared. 'Well, you'd better be quiet, boy, an' stay well in cover. That ain't no tenderfoot ahead.'

'I know how to handle myself,' stated Clute.

Simpson nodded. 'We'll see,' he said and padded into the trees. Clute Cross fell in behind him.

The shade of the trees was welcome. Close to their right, behind the greenery, Simpson could hear the stream gurgling and bubbling. It would be idyllic if their intentions hadn't been so deadly. Soon they entered a screen of willows. And while they were still in them Simpson saw the bushwhacker's horse lift its head. Sending a tingle up his spine it stared at them and whinnied. It was a dead giveaway.

Simpson went to earth. Clute went with him. Simpson scanned the gust-stirred screen of green ahead of him. There was still no movement up front. Then, from the corner of his eye, he saw Patter and three of the posse on foot like themselves, working their way up through the trees on the opposite side of the stream.

The grey moved again and snorted, this time looking at the possemen. Simpson began weaving his way out of the willows and into the tall grass. Cross stuck with him. Simpson could see the sweat running down the boy's face, could see the anxious, yet tense expectancy on his lean features.

Then a relieved shout came from the trees up ahead, 'Thank God. Marshal Patter.'

'Collins?' Though he couldn't see him, Simpson recognized Patter's puzzled enquiry. 'Now you hold real still, mister, an' throw that rifle of yours clear away from your body.'

'What the hell's gotten into you, Marshal?' came the protest. 'Damn it, I'm hit bad here. Got bushwhacked on the trail back there, but I managed to git clear of the sonofabitch.'

Patter rasped, 'You were *what?* Now somebody's got to be lyin' here.' With slight menace in his voice he added, 'You goin' to throw that piece aside, Montana?'

'Hell, if that bastard comes at me again, I want to be ready.'

'He won't. I promise you.'

There was muffled cursing. Then Patter said, 'That's better. Right, boys, move in. Keep your hands clear of that Colt, Montana.'

Simpson now saw the marshal and the three possemen step out of cover across the stream. They splashed through the creek's shallow depths and walked towards a copse of aspens a hundred yards ahead. From the grass beside him Clute Cross rose up. But Simpson wasn't ready for the rifle that jabbed into his back.

'You'd better throw down your rifle too, mister,' Cross said. 'Seems we got a heap of confusion here.'

Simpson rose slowly. 'Now take it easy, boy. That sonofabitch is lyin' through his back teeth.'

'Got on'y your word fer that. Now move toward the marshal.'

Simpson felt the rifle prod into his back again. Resenting it, he tensed. But maybe the boy was green enough to allow him to take a chance ...

He swung around quickly, dropping his own rifle and knocking Clute's aside before grasping it and wrenching it out of his hand. Simpson swallowed hard on his dry throat as he lined it up on the boy.

'Clute,' he said, letting his tension drain from him, 'sometimes, you've got to give a man a chance.'

'Nobody gave Pa one,' rasped the Cross boy, clearly startled and angered by the turn of events.

'Maybe not,' said Simpson. 'But on my oath, it weren't me that done it.'

'Agin. On'y your word fer that.'

'Move towards the marshal, Clute,' said Simpson, picking up his own rifle. 'But don't try any silly tricks.'

They threaded through the willow again

and came out into a clearing. Simpson saw Patter and his men clustered around a man sitting, his back leaning against a tree. Blood stained his left side. He looked pale and shocked. Simpson recognized him as one of the group who had backed Tranter at the M-M.

Patter turned as they broke out of the willows. The marshal's eyes narrowed when he saw the rifle trained on Clute.

'What goes, Simpson?' he demanded.

Simpson waved a hand. 'Clute here figured that sonofabitch may have shouted out the truth when he called out to you,' he said. 'He put his rifle on me. I had to relieve him of it.'

'Well, maybe he did hear the truth,' said Patter. 'Let the boy go, Simpson.'

Simpson shook his head, dropped Clute's rifle, lined up his own. 'Like to oblige. But that'll depend on what you got planned when I do that,' said Simpson. 'The whole thing was the way I told it, Patter. That man there is lyin'.'

Seeming to be bedevilled by the need for decision Patter ran a hand down the side of his chubby face, before he screwed it up. 'He's the one carryin' the bullet, not you,' he pointed out. 'Mebbe you saw him on your back trail and laid up for him. I know Tranter won't have taken kind to you shootin' one of his men an' maybe set him on to you.'

'That sonofabitch killed my horse,' growled Simpson. 'Just for that, I ought to drill him here an' now.'

'Mebbe he figured that was the on'y way to stop you, shot up as he was,' countered Patter. 'I reckon if it really was Montana that laid in the bushes waitin' you'd have been dead now, mister. Collins allus reckons he's one of the best riflemen in the basin.'

'I got lucky,' explained Simpson. 'He sent up a couple of birds and I guessed somebody was holed up ahead, waitin' for me.' But Simpson found his pulses had begun to race. He began to appreciate that, to the suspicious mind, this didn't look good. 'You gotta believe that, Marshal.'

Patter shook his round head. 'I gotta believe nothin', Simpson, you should know that—ex-lawman an' all. I have to go on what is told me and what evidence I can uncover, then I gotta make a calculated guess until I get concrete proof. Cover him, boys.'

Abruptly, Patter swung up his rifle along with the three possemen strung around him. Simpson's gut tightened up. There was also the possemen back down the draw who could make this even more difficult. Then Patter fired two shots into the air. Had to be a signal, Simpson decided.

With equal rapidity, he stepped forward and put his arm around Clute's neck, lined up Clute's rifle. 'I'm sorry about this, boy,' he said in the youngest Cross's ear. Now he glared at Patter. 'I don't want this, Marshal. But I can't find out nothin' shacked up in jail, if that's what you're figurin' to do.'

'I'll see you get a fair trial,' said Patter.

Strangely, Simpson found himself believing that. But he rasped, 'Sorry I can't test that, Patter.' He swung the rifle from side to side. 'Now, if nobody moves, nobody gets hurt.'

But arousing a measure of desperation in him, Simpson heard the pound of hooves coming up the draw. Had to be the rest of the posse.

'Give yourself up, Simpson,' Patter called urgently. 'We don't want more blood spilt.'

Carl stared around him anxiously. Montana Collins's horse, once more cropping grass by the stream, he realized, was his one chance. It looked a sound beast that could have plenty of running in it. He tugged Clute with him, using his body as a shield as he moved towards it. The boy struggled, but Simpson held him with an iron-muscled arm.

'Don't do it, Simpson,' warned Patter, stepping forward. There was a hint of urgency in his voice, pleading even. 'Let the boy go and raise your arms.'

Ignoring Patter and reaching the horse, Simpson said, 'Take the reins, boy. Lead him.'

Now Patter recommended, 'Do it, Clute! Don't try an' be brave.'

To Simpson's relief, Clute obliged.

'Into those trees, boy,' he said, holding on to him.

Clute moved. Simpson backed with him and moved into the trees, fanning the rifle in his hand from side to side as he went, covering the posse. The other posse members now pounded into the clearing.

Patter raised his arms. 'Easy, boys,' he warned anxiously. 'Let him do what he figures to do. We'll git him when Clute's safe.'

'Move into the trees, boy,' breathed Simpson. 'An' easy. Just remember, there ain't nothin' to die for here.'

A posseman raised his Colt. Simpson

blasted a shot that kicked up dirt at the man's feet.

'God damn—hold it,' raged Patter at the trigger-happy posseman.

As soon as Simpson figured he had enough trees between him to give him a real chance, he unhooked Clute's Colt from its holster and hurled it into the bushes, then let go of him and swung up.

'I didn't kill your pa, boy,' he muttered as a parting shot, 'but I'm sure as hell goin' to try my damnedest to find out who did, an' a whole lot of other things.' He kicked flanks and raced up the draw.

Clute Cross stared after him, relieved to have got out of this with no hurt, and feeling, despite the indignity he had suffered, there was something about Carl Simpson a man had to trust, like it or not.

EIGHT

Marshal John Patter was none too sure of his emotions as he watched Simpson mount up and kick the big grey gelding belonging to Montana Collins into a gallop up the draw towards the Midanbar Canyon.

He saw Clute Cross duck and head out of the line of fire he seemed sure was about to commence. Running wide Clute gradually came back to join the posse. A ragged roll of rifle fire sent lead snarling savagely through the trees, tearing white wood and ripping leaves off the boughs that got in the way.

'Hold it, boys,' roared Patter. 'You're wastin' lead.'

'You goin' after him?' demanded Coke Hewson. His black stare was searching.

There was something about Coke Hewson Patter had never liked. Hewson had a cabin in the Pecons and hunted for a living, bringing the game he shot into Hell to sell. He also got contracts from the ranchers to kill cougars, coyotes and wolves when they became too much of a nuisance. He'd happened to be in town when the news of the deaths of Cross and his two hands came in and had volunteered his services. Patter found that unusual for a start, for Hewson liked to get paid for his involvement in anything like this. More than once he'd brought men in for the price on their heads, usually dead.

'One thing at a damned time, Hewson,' said Patter irately. He hated to be rushed. 'Sure we're goin' after him, but there's Montana here to consider. He's hit bad.'

He turned to Saul Pollard of Pollard's Emporium. 'You put the first aid equipment in those saddle-bags like I asked?'

Pollard nodded, but looked angry, as if resenting the tone of the question. 'Sure I did. But I want payin' fer it.'

Patter stared fiercely. 'You'll git your damned money. Bein' head of the town council I reckon you'll make damn sure o' that.'

The fact that this was all going wrong was beginning to irritate Patter immensely. First off, all he was was a damned town marshal, nothing more. He should have kept his nose out, but knew he couldn't. He'd been a frontier lawman for too many years, got his training along the border with the Rangers.

But hit with the marshal's words Pollard glared some more and Patter wished the grousing sonofabitch had never chosen to ride with the posse. He began to figure all the man saw in the chase was next Fall's votes.

Then, 'I got some experience with wounds durin' the war,' volunteered Coke Hewson. Patter engaged the hunter's cold, black stare. 'But more to the point,' Hewson was going on calmly, 'when

I've fixed up Collins, you still goin' after Simpson?'

Marshal Patter narrowed his gaze. Try as he might, he'd never been able to trust this swarthy, sombre hunter. There had always been an aura of bad about him. 'Coke, I want him brought in whole, y'hear? I want no killin'. I ain't sure he's guilty. I want to talk to Taw McAdam, see if Simpson's story holds up about him bein' with Taw when Abel an' his boys were shot.'

Hewson opened his mouth to reply but Montana Collins moaned from his position, propped against the cottonwood. 'Hell, ain't somebody goin' to pad up this hole? I'm leakin' like a damned tap here.'

Patter growled, 'Well, you goin' to see to Montana, Coke?'

Hewson glared. 'I said I would, didn't I?'

With that Patter decided he'd never liked Hewson's mean features, either. And it remained to be seen what Hewson knew about first aid. And there was something about Hewson's black stare—the way it fastened on to a man like grappling hooks, holding him and examining him before letting him go. It could be intimidating ... if you let it be. And this sudden swell of human kindness oozing from the man didn't fit. There must be some motive behind it.

Hewson's hard look button-holed him now. 'I'm just wantin' to know—are you goin' to put a price on this man Simpson? Judgin' by the feelin' in town this morning, a lot o' folks think he is guilty as hell an' would agree to a bounty.'

Patter shook his head emphatically. He'd already figured Hewson would eventually get round to that and wanted to stall him. 'I've no authority,' he said. 'The town council will have to decide that.'

Coke Hewson pursed his thin, knife-scar-deformed lips. 'You got Pollard here, head of the damned council. He can sanction it. But I reckon Bart Tranter'll come up with a price, seein' as how two of his riders have been hit by Simpson. I figure he won't need to run to any committee to put a price on a man. My guess is he'll figure Simpson a number one priority an' he won't be fussed about him bein' dead, or alive, when he's brung in.'

'Simpson claims he was defendin' himself against those two,' came back Patter. 'I'm inclined to believe him.'

Hewson grinned wolfishly. 'I guess that won't cut much ice with Tranter, though,' he said smoothly. 'Now he's a real mean sonofabitch when he wants to be. An' I guess, right now, he wants to be.'

Still smiling ghoulishly Hewson took the saddlebag with the first aid equipment in it that Saul Pollard passed to him and crouched down beside the groaning Collins. Over his shoulder the hunter said, 'My guess also is, Tranter'll say five hundred dollars an' kill him.' He spat chew juice. 'Well, hell, I'd like a slice of *that* action.'

Patter scowled at Hewson's back. 'Damn

it, Hewson, this is a man's life we're talkin' about.'

Hewson cut away Montana's shirt, examined the wound. 'You runnin' outa sand in your old age, Patter?' he said. 'Man, wolf, what's the difference if the sonofabitch is runnin' around tryin' to kill people?' He went quiet while he looked at Collins's wound. Then he said, 'I reckon the bullet missed anythin' vital, Montana, though you've lost a deal of blood. But, barrin' infection, you'll make it.' He commenced padding the wound and bandaging it up.

As he watched Hewson work Patter rubbed his chin, which was rough with dark, day-old bristles, then preened his moustache. He attempted to brush aside his forebodings concerning Hewson. First off, somebody had to take Montana Collins on to the Boxed T. He'd considered taking him to the M-M for a moment, which was nearer, then thought that wouldn't be very sensible, taking in the hostility developing between the two brands just now.

A pang of anger bit at Patter. Damn it, he was a *town* marshal. Strictly speaking, this was county work. Why should he find himself doing it? But at root he was a lawman first and Cross had been a friend, a close friend, and that made the difference. However, most of this going on now wasn't about Abel and his dead punchers. It was about Simpson whittling away at the Boxed T.

He felt inclined to firmly believe Simpson's claim that Montana Collins *had* been lying in wait for him, simply because he, too, had been a lawman and a good one. He'd heard nothing good about Collins since he'd come into the basin. Collins had proved to be an arrogant bastard, always boasting about his prowess with that fancy rifle he carried, though he was never ready to prove it, always saying come the Fourth of July celebrations, when the yearly shooting contest was organized along with the horse racing, he'd show everybody then how good he was and not before.

Patter narrowed his eyes. Now that would sure settle it if Collins really was as good as he claimed to be, or it would shut him up for good if he wasn't. Patter had to confess to his own mind he'd been eagerly awaiting the event, just to see Collins eat crow. There were some good riflemen in the basin, Coke Hewson for one.

'I figure to take Collins to the Boxed T,' Hewson said, rising from beside the wounded man, the dressing job done. 'Rig up some sort of a travois to take him in on.'

Patter stared at the hunter keenly. 'I'd like you with the posse, Hewson,' he said. He thought, *where I can keep an eye on you.*

Hewson grinned with knife-scarred lips. It was more a leer. 'Hell, you don't need me. You an' young Clute can read sign 'bout as good as me.'

'Well, I'll speak on behalf of the town

council,' piped up Saul Pollard, who'd been hovering round, listening to the conversation. 'I'll put two hundred dollars on Simpson's head if you'll take on the job from here, Hewson. Me and most of the riders here have families to go back to. I don't figure to stay on this all night.'

'Handsome,' said Hewson, 'but I'd just like to hear what kind of money Tranter has to offer first.'

Patter felt his gut tighten, and anger burn in him after Pollard's intervention. 'If you do this alone, Hewson, I want that man brought in alive, y' hear?'

Hewson spread his hands, attempting as much innocence as he was capable of. 'I hear. An' if he acts sensible an' don't git to shootin', he will be. If he don't,' Hewson pursed his lips, 'well, I gotta defend myself. But we're all jumpin' gun here, ain't we? Most likely, soon as I've delivered Collins here, I'll be on your back trail, hopin' to catch up an' help out.'

Patter stared with hard eyes. 'I'd like

that plenty.' But he put warning in his tone and saw that Hewson had picked it up. It only prompted a slow, scornful grin.

The hunter went off to cut poles for his travois.

Patter growled, turned to Clute Cross. 'Boy,' he said, 'can you get some coffee an' vittles goin?' He stared through the trees at the massive ochre maw that was the Midanbar Canyon Simpson had disappeared into. 'I figure this could turn out to be a long haul.'

NINE

It was past noon when Coke Hewson rode into the Boxed T confines with Montana Collins behind him on the improvised travois he'd constructed. Bart Tranter, standing on the stoop, could only stare at him, his sharp features drawn, his amber stare brittle.

'What in the hell ...?' he growled.

Hewson grinned wolfishly at him. 'Guess your boy didn't get the job done, Tranter.'

The Boxed T boss glared. 'What're you suggestin', Hewson?'

Hewson spat juice. 'Well, Montana here said Simpson shot at him from ambush,' explained Hewson. He climbed down stiffly from his horse. The early afternoon sun was fierce and unforgiving, though it was beginning to dip towards the Pecon Hills miles to the west, beyond the mesas and canyons. Hewson mopped his wrinkled brow with a dirty rag. 'But Simpson explained Montana did the bushwhackin', but failed the attempt an' paid for it with his lead. Now, I figure, since Cole Harkness took lead off Simpson as well you might have plotted to get ...'

'You're figurin' too much, Hewson,' cut in Tranter coldly. 'Speculating about things that ain't your concern, that could get you into a heap of trouble.'

'With two of your best boys failin',' went on Hewson, untroubled by Tranter's veiled aggression, 'I reckon I can mebbe root out an' kill that sonofabitch for you ... at the right price. Seems, for some reason, you want him bad.'

The owner of the Boxed T's look was hawkish. 'You figure, huh?' he growled.

At ease, Hewson nodded, fished out his plug and shaved a cud off it, spat out the old and shoved in the new, tucking the wad in his left cheek. 'You want him dead, don't you?' he said.

Taken off balance for a moment, Tranter stared moodily at the mesas and canyons south-west. He had the rest of his hardcases in Ellis Canyon, laying dynamite right now. He'd teach McAdam, fencing off his damned water. And sure he wanted Simpson dead. Including Harkness, Collins's failure made two useless sonsofbitches on his payroll and both plugged with Simpson's lead. Tranter's law demanded retribution. However, it wasn't only that—what rankled most was his own judgement of men seemed to have fallen off bad recently.

Damn it, he'd have liked to have killed off that sonofabitch Simpson himself, now he'd had the opportunity placed in his lap. But he wanted to get it out of the way quick. There were other more pressing matters than Simpson. Even so, though those Mostens had never amounted to much with him, they *were* kin. Blood must be paid for with blood. It went right back to the upbringing they'd all had in the Appalachians. Family honour was all. But, at the moment, there were bigger fish frying. The control of this basin. Simpson had to take second place. But, Tranter thought, he still wanted it done. And maybe, now, he'd got the man to do it. The decision came swiftly.

'O'Rourke, Pinner,' he bellowed. Two men came out of the saddle room. Old, near-crippled hands, used for doing all the chores around the ranch. Cleaning out, saddle mending ... they had come with the spread when he had bought it. He should have finished them, like he had most of the other hands, when he brought in his own men. But they had proved useful doing the menial chores and they were both *South*, both wounded at Little Round Top in the Gettysburg shindig. Even though they'd been run off that damned hill, that had touched what few chords of humanity he had left and they'd stayed.

He met Pinner's grey squint as the two

men came close. 'You want somethin', Mr Tranter?' the puncher said.

The Boxed T boss waved a hand. 'Get Collins down to the bunkhouse. See to his needs.' He turned to Hewson. 'You, come into the house.'

The two hands lifted Collins, who was now unconscious, and carried him away.

Hewson detached the makeshift travois from his horse. Free of its encumbrance he tied the mount to the rail in front of the long, low adobe ranch-house and followed the owner of the Boxed T into the coolness of the dwelling.

Inside Tranter poured two large whiskies, handed one to Hewson. 'You figure you can get the job done?' he said.

Hewson took a sip of whiskey, then said, 'Patter an' his posse are after him. He's gone into Midanbar Canyon. I reckon those greenhorns'll find nothin'. Saul Pollard an' some of the other citizens of Hell are already claimin' they've done more'n enough an' are wantin' to git back.

Patter has on'y himself an' young Clute Cross with any real trailin' experience, so it could all peter out purty quick. I figure if I move fast, I can meet Simpson as he finds his way out of the north exit.'

Excited by Hewson's cold assessment, Tranter nodded. He had always suspected there was the potential to be a mankiller in Hewson, if that wasn't already the case. He suspected there'd been a time when Hewson hadn't always hunted just animals for a living. It was in the eyes. Dead, dark and brooding. He'd seen that killer look in many a man's eye in the war. 'Want to know why I want him dead?' he said.

Hewson shook his head. 'Less I know, the easier it is. You want the job done, Mr Tranter ... well, if the money is right, I'll git it done for you.'

'How does two hundred dollars sound?'

Hewson pursed his scarred lips. 'Don't have much of a ring to it. I thought you wanted Simpson stronger than that.'

Tranter's gaze set hard. 'Four hundred

an' fifty when the job's done.'

Hewson raised thin brows. 'I was thinkin' more like three hundred now, two hundred when I've laid Simpson to rest.'

Tranter glared, took a swig of the whiskey in his hand. 'By God, you fancy yourself. How do I know you won't just take off outa here when I hand the money over?'

'You don't,' said Hewson. 'But I figure, readin' the sign developin' in this basin, you'll mebbe need more work done from the bushes purty soon an' you're already findin' you ain't got the men to do it. I figure if I do real good on this one, there might be other work. An' no shit on your doorstep.'

'What do you mean?'

'I mean, I was on the trail last night when you bushwhacked Cross an' his boys. I saw it all. It was a messy job.'

Tranter's stare turned evil. 'So, you wantin' me to buy your silence?' He appended, 'If I did it, that is.'

Hewson smiled, without humour. 'Hell, no. Like I said, all I want is a piece of the action.'

Tranter looked at the sallow-faced hunter, the coldness in his eye. A new respect grew in him. This was a man who could be very useful. And maybe his choice of men would take a turn for the better if he followed it up. He'd never been a man to shirk a quick decision when one was needed.

He nodded. 'OK. No shit on my doorstep ... understood? An' if you play it as though you're still doin' your job bringin' in fresh game, better still. When I have a job, I'll send for you. And if the one you do on Simpson is satisfactory ... maybe I can even think of upping the ante on the others—McAdam, for instance.'

Hewson smiled, his knife-scarred, ghoulish smile. 'I think we'll get on real well, Mr Tranter.' Warming with satisfaction, the hunter lifted his glass, saluted Tranter and drank its contents. His thoughts were cynical: Pollard could peddle his two hundred dollars somewhere else ...

TEN

Screened by the trees in the draw Carl Simpson rode fast and hard atop Collins's big grey, away from Patter's posse. He found the horse under him was a lively beast which suggested it might have ample stamina. But as he rode he realized the canyon he had galloped into was vast, the rock within it carved into crumbling pillars and buttes that stood up in red and ochre columns from the canyon floor. And any trail he plotted had to wind around and between these silent sentinels and through sprawls of lower ground greasewood and pine, with fir clumped on the higher slopes. It appeared to him at first glance that there was no way out ahead. In fact, it seemed to him he had run slap bang into a box canyon.

He had been puzzled by the lack of immediate pursuit, now he was beginning to appreciate why. It suggested they knew there was no way out and could take their time.

He stared ahead, eyes desperately searching the rugged terrain. There were a dozen places he could see, all made for ambush. Well that could work for him as well as Patter and his posse. But he didn't want that. In fact, that was the last thing he wanted. He wanted Patter and his men on his side, and young Clute Cross. Shooting at them wouldn't be a very clever thing to do, that was for sure.

Then there was Coke Hewson. Now there was a mean character, he was beginning to appreciate. A hunter for sure and not only of animals. His instinct told him that. Simpson chewed on his upper lip. He'd had that breed call on him during his days as Territorial Marshal, looking for high-paying Wanted dodgers. All they had ever seemed interested in was the price on a man's head, and knew only one way to bring him in. That was dead. Would Patter be able to hold him? Hewson would definitely be his own man. But Simpson had a gnawing feeling in him telling him that Hewson would need dollars before he'd put any real enthusiasm into tracking him down. Until that was forthcoming ...

Simpson felt a small comfort in that. Far as he knew, there'd been no dollars put on him, yet. So the best he could hope for now was that the townspeople in the posse would win out with their arguments to return to Hell, and that Hewson would be denied his dollars. Meanwhile, he had to figure a way of avoiding Patter and find a way of getting out of this canyon. Simpson took a draft of water from his canteen.

Leaving the Boxed T, terms agreed, Coke Hewson travelled fast. Late afternoon found him sitting amongst the pines on the castellated north edge of the spectacular

Midanbar Canyon and peering down into its vastness. He'd ridden hard from the ranch to get here. He set his German binoculars—taken off a Prussian officer he'd killed in the North–South conflict—to his black, narrowed eyes and probed the men enveloped in the bubble of dust way down there on the heat-tortured floor.

It was Patter's posse.

He was surprised they were still together. He had expected them to break up sooner than this. Three solid meals a day and a comparatively easy life behind a counter, or whatever, didn't usually equip a man for the deprivations to be experienced down in that hell-hole. Most of them had families, too. They would be wanting to get back to them sure enough.

Hewson grinned wolfishly. It shouldn't be long before they did break up, he decided, even though it would take them all night to get back to Hell. And that left the one thing to concern him: Simpson. After half an hour of searching with the binoculars he had yet to find him. If he was moving down there, he wasn't raising much dust.

Hewson moved the lenses he had to his eyes, methodically searching the shimmering ochre bottomland and dramatically shelved walls. Then he stopped. There, on the plateau in that high clump of trees, halfway up the side of the canyon. Movement. He juggled with the focus wheel in an attempt to sharpen the image more. It was Collins's big grey horse, the one Simpson had lit out on. It was tethered in brush, cropping at the meagre grass that grew there. But still no Simpson.

Sonofabitch! Hewson returned his gaze to the dust enveloping the posse. He felt sure that Simpson hadn't seen the posse yet, assuming he was near his horse, but it wouldn't be long before he did. He was in a very good position to. Hewson then decided Simpson's plan would probably be to sit there and let the riders move right past him, then he would make off, back down the trail again and out of the canyon, not knowing there was an outlet ahead of him. Hewson nodded. That's what he personally would do if he was in Simpson's shoes. He thought Simpson would be experienced enough to think that way, too.

He lowered the binoculars slowly and smiled for the truth of it was, he knew, *there was a way out*. However, it'd take nerve on the part of Simpson, or contempt for the quality of the posse, to attempt the move he suspected he might make, for nobody should underestimate Patter. He'd been a lawdog of one sort and another for a long time, that much Hewson was sure of.

But if Simpson could work his way out of this and get back on to the range again, it would be more difficult to keep track of him—not impossible, but difficult. And, thought Hewson, why make things more complicated?

He pulled his knife-scarred lips. He had

to keep Simpson under his gun, and he had to get him before he rode out of Midanbar Canyon. And south was the place where he would have to try if his hunch was correct.

Down below, Marshal John Patter wiped the sweat from his furrowed brow. God, but it was damned hot. He stared momentarily at the sun now moving down towards the red, castellated western edges of the immense rim of the canyon he was in. One thought bothered him. Where in Hades was Simpson? The man couldn't know this canyon, its twists and turns, its hidden exit to the north. Patter admitted to himself he didn't know it all that well himself.

'I'm getting fed up with this,' Saul Pollard protested. Patter saw Pollard's pin-striped suit was dust-laden and patched dark with sweat. He was clearly suffering badly from the heat. Salt around the edges of the perspiration marks showed white.

And his derby hat, tilted forward, was completely out of place in this situation. 'I think we should leave the whole damn business to Hewson,' he grumbled on. He nodded his small head to express his conviction. Its roundness was now reddened by the sun and sheened heavily with exudation. His stone grey eyes were like pebbles in their small sockets. 'If I know Hewson at all he'll rise to the bait of two hundred dollars, never fear.'

'That's why we've got to get to Simpson first,' growled Patter. He was getting sick and fed up with Pollard's griping, and some of the others in the posse that were putting in their two cents' worth. 'If we don't, Hewson will kill him. You made a damn fool mistake when you offered him money.'

Pollard stared indignantly. 'I don't think so. That man Simpson's too handy with a gun to merit much concern. And we don't know for sure that he *didn't* lie in wait for Montana Collins and put a bullet in him, or did for Cross and his boys.' Pollard wagged a righteous finger. 'He who lives by the sword, must surely die, by the sword.'

Patter sighed wearily. 'Shut up, Saul,' he growled. 'Damn it, if this ain't suitin' you, ride on back to Hell. You should reach the town by dawn.'

'I'm not prepared to ride my horse into the ground,' countered Pollard hotly. 'And I think we should hold together. This Simpson, seeing a man on his own, might attempt to ambush him, just as surely as he did Montana.'

Patter glared. 'You keep sayin' it. We don't know he did. And I for one, sure figure he didn't. So fer Christ's sake, Saul, will you shut up? Sound carries a hell of a way down here. Simpson'll hear us coming a mile away.'

Pollard stared irately, wagged another finger. 'Now look here, John,' he began, arching his thin brows. The general goods store owner then seemed to run out of words as Patter's gaze now turned hostile and menacing.

'Well, maybe you're right,' he muttered sulkily. He slumped down in the saddle and wiped the back of his neck and momentarily grimaced at the sun, defeated as much by their situation as Patter's strength of character.

During the exchange Carl Simpson took another short drink from the canteen he had found on Montana Collins's saddle and wiped his mouth with the back of his hand. Patter and his posse had just come into view. He allowed himself a wry grin. They looked a sorry bunch. But his humour didn't last long. He appreciated he was in a serious position here. And there was another thing: half an hour ago, on the northern rimrock, he had seen a momentary flash of sun on metal—he was positive it wasn't the glint of water. Now, with the posse in view and discernible, he saw Hewson was not amongst their ranks.

And putting two and two together, if Simpson knew anything at all, he'd lay money Hewson knew this country like the back of his hand. And thinking more on it, it was a strong possibility it was him on the rimrock. If he'd been made a bounty offer, that was where he would head. Like the eagle, it would give him a big advantage to be able to gaze down on all that was happening below, then he could pick his time and pick his place. Who had supplied the money to give him a full interest in this was beside the point at the moment.

Now diverting Simpson, in the bottom of the canyon he saw Clute Cross pause, talk to Patter. Clute had been slightly ahead of the posse, studying the ground. Simpson accepted he had found his tracks and was following the trail he had left, though he had strived to make it as difficult as possible. But the canyon bottom was loose soil and grit, making it hard to hide his tracks.

The boy seemed to know what he

was looking for. Both he and Patter now scanned the narrow plateau he had ascended to in the hope they would pass him and he would be able to back-trail out of this place. He realized immediately he had underestimated them. Damn.

He watched Patter take out his telescope, begin searching the screen of pine he was using as cover. The horse was all right, further back on this shelf, in a small clearing cropping the thin grass there. He would not be picked out.

Then Patter bellowed, surprising him, 'Simpson! Come out an' we'll talk. I don't think you want shootin' here any more than I do.'

The demand was faint because of the distance but clear enough. And Simpson thought, damned right I don't want shooting. But he for certain knew Patter would maintain his insistence that he should give himself up and let the law take its course if he did decide to break cover. However, Simpson determined, being behind bars in Hell's pokey jailhouse was not going to help him solve the things going on in this basin, for he had fully decided to do that. He'd been shot at, his horse killed.

He remained still and silent. But while he did he made a more thorough survey of the narrow plateau he was on. He had to find a way out along it if he could. Doubling back was not a realistic ambition any more. But being where he was gave him some time to play with. It would be a long, hard climb for Patter and his posse, if they were going to come up the canyon side after him. And they were going to have to do it cautiously because they couldn't be certain Simpson would not fire down on them. He decided, all in all, if things broke, he'd have a comfortable lead. But he mustn't be smug. That could be fatal.

Simpson rubbed his chin, then ran a scan of the northern rim, the vicinity where he had seen the brief glint of dull light. There was danger up there, too—maybe even greater than he faced down here, of that he was sure. Marshal Patter was out to take him in and purely that, but if it was Hewson up there, at a rough guess, he would be out to take him any which way it called for. Most likely, dead. And Hewson would maybe be thinking Carl Simpson was not about to give himself up to anybody, either—Coke Hewson in particular—and that would almost certainly cause lead to fly to settle it between them.

Simpson shifted his gaze further upwards, to the sky. The sun was now approaching the western rim of the canyon. Soon it would dip behind it and darkness would gather in this deep place. He had to hold out long enough, then strive to use its cover to escape.

'Simpson! You hear me?' Patter's voice came floating up the rugged stony slope again to reach him faintly. He could see Patter was leaning forward aggressively. It could only be with angry frustration.

Again Simpson scanned the place he had seen the glint. To get around to there from here would take a rider the better part of an hour or more, if he knew the terrain. He didn't, but he felt sure that man up there knew it. And, right now, he clearly knew the best place to be to view the whole of the canyon. And maybe, because he was where he was, there was *a way out of here up there.* Simpson blinked at the result of his deduction, but it would maybe take him right under that bastard's gun, unless he was thinking the way he himself had originally thought: that he would back-track. Simpson narrowed his eyelids. And if he was ...

Simpson realized it was decision time. Adopt the original plan of back-tracking, or head out towards the place he had seen the reflection. And that set his thought processes working overtime. Yes, Hewson—if it *was* him up there—would maybe figure that would be his, Simpson's, plan: head back out of the canyon the way he had come, if he could fool Patter. It would make the most sense to a man who didn't know the terrain, but had been around a little. Maybe that was how Hewson would be thinking.

Simpson scrubbed his determined chin once more, licked his dry lips and then wiped globules of sweat off his high forehead. Man, oh, man, how had he gotten into this? It was all maybes. And the wrong maybe could cost him his life.

He looked down at Patter and his posse again. They were in what appeared to be heated discussion. It went on for half a minute or more, then Patter turned his horse and began to urge it cautiously up the slope towards the plateau. Clute Cross was half a horse behind him. The rest of the posse followed on, but clearly very reluctantly.

Simpson withdrew from the edge of the narrow plateau. He could see it extended for two miles or more north, at times going behind ranks of eroded pinnacles of stone.

There were places where it would need great care not to expose his position—both to Patter and the man on the rimrock, if he was still scanning for him.

Simpson then gathered Collins's horse, and began to pick his way along the route he had mapped out, using the pine screen. The going was rough, boulder-strewn, needing many diversions. At one point, he had to edge his way along the lip of the plateau, though he was covered by a bank of rock from the eyes of the posse. But he could not avoid the clatter of loose rock that was dislodged by nervous hooves when he did. The debris rattled and bounced its way down for a thousand feet before it joined a huge bed of shale below that had sheared off over the years.

He glanced behind him. He saw Patter emerging from the tortuous slope he had had to climb to get to where he obviously suspected Simpson was. The rattle of stones sent him scurrying back down under the protection of the lip of the plateau again, calling to the posse to do likewise.

Again, faintly because of the distance between them, Patter's roar came, 'Be sensible, Simpson. Give it up. There's a blank wall up there.'

Bluff? Simpson found his mind racing once more. He stared ahead. For sure, he couldn't see a way out of the north end of this place yet. But hunch and instinct and approaching darkness urged him to carry on. He based his decision solely on the assumption that the man behind the glint of glass up there knew there was a way out ahead. Thing was, would he be waiting for him to find it and make his way through it, or would he have figured he might have back-tracked? Simpson felt a wave of anxiety, but he pressed on. There was only one way to find out.

ELEVEN

Coke Hewson realized his mistake quickly. He had been skirting the western rim of the canyon, heading for the south exit to wait for Simpson. But a pause and a quick scan with the glasses told him instead of Marshal Patter passing Simpson; he had picked up his trail and was driving him to the north end. And there, Hewson felt sure, Simpson would find the gap that would take him out of the canyon.

He tugged viciously on the rein and swung his big horse around. He could have cursed to hell and gone, but he didn't. He'd made an educated guess; it had turned out the wrong one, all due to that damned marshal down there and maybe young Cross. Now he had a task on. He had to get to the north gap before

Simpson did. It was a tall order, and with night closing down fast it would complicate matters.

Greed caused his black eyes to glitter. But five hundred dollars for Simpson's head and maybe more to come, he'd be a damned fool not to give it his best shot. He urged his horse on with a cruel rake of the spurs.

When he got to the steep gap that was the only trail north out of Midanbar Canyon it was nearly dark. Already the stars showed in the darkening sky and the cold of this high place was closing in on him. He shucked into his sheepskin. Inspection of the stony ground told him a horseman had been through here and not too long ago. His coal-black stare hardened. Simpson, the sonofabitch, had beaten him to it.

He stared up at the tree line crowning the top of the ridge that took the trail on to the Boxed T range and out of the canyon, then he kneed his mount and sent it up the trail. If he could just get a sight of Simpson, the direction he was going, that would help. But he knew it was unlikely. And the firs up there stretched for a mile or more into the Boxed T range before thinning out. Simpson would take full advantage of that. Hewson narrowed his mean eyes. When the near-full moon showed, it was going to need a lot of slow, patient work to find Simpson, but it could be done. Meantime it wouldn't hurt to get over the ridge and wait a while. More so when he heard the noise of Patter's posse far below coming up the long, twisting trail. He, sure as hell, didn't want the posse's company right now. But it was a more than even bet when they got through the gap the posse would give up for the night, make camp and take up the chase in the morning.

Grim-faced, heart pulsing, Simpson eased back into the dense tree cover as he watched Hewson pick his way towards him up the slope. He had watched the hunter come off the western rim that joined with the sunken, eroded wall through which the gap cut a path.

While he had waited it had become dark and cool and during that time he had formed a new plan. He'd guessed, from what he had heard while at the M-M and with the posse, that to continue to head north would take him on to Bart Tranter's land. That wouldn't help. He wanted to get to the McAdams' spread. Things were boiling up mighty fast against him here and that was the only place he could reasonably expect to get assistance, for he now reckoned he was in bad need of some.

So the scheme was, let Hewson and Patter's posse go past him—for some time he'd heard the posse faintly clattering about down there—then make his way back through the canyon and on to the M-M range. He'd have to hope that was the last thing they would expect him to do. It was a fact that most fugitives, in the first heat of the chase, just wanted to put space between themselves and their pursuers. It would be thought unlikely he would turn and go right past them. At least, that's what he hoped they would figure. But Hewson had to be the rogue card in the hand. However, maybe even *he* could be fooled for a while, long enough for Simpson to put some distance between himself and the hunter. Maybe even, he was giving the man too much respect. But gut-felt caution, instinct, perhaps, told Simpson that it would be a mistake not to.

He tensed. Hewson was close now. Shallowing his breathing Simpson pressed his horse's nose, stopping it calling to Hewson's. It remained to be seen what Hewson's big mount would do. Simpson had already got downwind but up here, in the gap, the breeze was capricious and could turn quickly. It didn't and Hewson went past him now no more than a dark shadow of horse and rider.

Relieved, Simpson waited for the posse. Ten minutes later, it went past noisily. He could hear Saul Pollard grumbling and Patter growling back at him. Somebody asked, 'Damn it, when we goin' to eat? Can't pick up a damned trail in this dark.'

'We'll get through the gap, first.' That was Patter. 'Come moonlight, we could pick out the trail.'

'The trail, always the damned trail,' Simpson heard Pollard rasp. 'But, God damn it, I'm getting to have the need to see this thing through to the bitter end. Call it just plain cussedness if you like.'

Patter said, sounding clearly relieved, 'Now you're talkin', Saul. An' I call it grit.'

Surprised, too, by the sudden infusion of steel in Saul Pollard, Simpson gave the posse a minute or two to clear the skyline, then urged Collins's grey back down the trail into the dark deeps of the Midanbar Canyon.

TWELVE

Taw McAdam felt drained as he walked his horse into the confines of the M-M. The ranch-house and bunkhouse were in darkness. It had taken him the best part of four hours to ride across the basin from the Circle C.

The big moon overhead would have made it a pleasant ride had he not been so tired and worried. Worried for Lucy, worried about the shooting of Abel Cross and his hands, worried about the welfare of Carl Simpson, worried about Pa and his run in with Tranter and wondering if the two—the deaths of Cross and his two punchers—were linked with Tranter and Pa was next. Up until now, such concern would have been alien to him. He'd been helling around the last couple of years, without much of a care for anything except his own enjoyment. Nothing serious bad, but irritating to a lot of folk. Now ... like Pa said, it was time he started to do some growing.

He unsaddled the bay he had picked out of the remuda for the ride to the Circle C. He'd walked her the last couple of miles to cool her down. He rough-groomed her, led her to the corral and tossed her hay before heading for the ranch-house and much needed sleep.

But the sound of a load being jacked into a Winchester behind him had him spinning and reaching for the Colt at his hip, whipping it up and cocking it.

'Easy, Taw,' came the urgent call. 'Just joshin'.'

In the strong moonlight he saw Marty Graham, youngest of the M-M punchers, rifle in hand, but hanging loosely, down by his side. He must have been in the shadows of the barn, bunkered down behind that old wagon wheel. Damn it,

Marty was even grinning.

'You tryin' to scare the shit outa me, Marty?' he rumbled. 'God damn it, I could have shot you. Things ain't purty around here right now. You recall that?'

Marty wiped the grin off his face and said, 'Hell, ol' sober sides fer onc't? But I guess you're right. This ain't the time fer such foolin'. As fer me bein' here, your pa thought it best he posted lookouts for a day or two, way things are with the Boxed T.'

'Still don't say you've got to scare the shit outa *me*,' repeated Taw irately. He stormed off towards the house. Marty Graham had a sense of humour that would get him killed some day, he decided on the way. It never occurred to him that his was in similar vein.

Inside the house he wolfed down some cold beef he found in the kitchen then headed for his bedroom at the far end of the long passage, the passage that linked the living spaces and bedrooms of the

M-M dwelling house.

Without bothering to undress, bone tired as he was having had no sleep for near forty-eight hours, he flopped on to the iron-framed bed. Within seconds he was breathing easily, the cares of the world forgotten.

But while Taw slept, deep in Ellis Canyon, where the ochre faces of the chasm narrowed to make it less than fifty yards across, and where the water ran out of the base of the rock wall to form a large, deep pool before flowing away towards the M-M, Bart Tranter stared at the bunch of hardcases around him. They were grouped behind boulders, away from the west rim of the canyon. The rolls of dynamite they had wedged into the overhang, primed and wired, were now awaiting the press of the plunger under the Boxed T boss's large hand.

Tranter's grin was wolfish as he gazed around the faces of his men. 'Well, here's an end to McAdam's game,' he growled.

He pressed the plunger.

The roar of the detonation crashed across the moon-silvered solitude of the big range, banging echoes down the canyon, then across the basin and into the Pecon Hills beyond. The clatter and rumble of rock, falling like a shower of gigantic hail, completed the calamity of noise before it yammered away into silence. Only dust rose in a huge pall now from the canyon's depths before drifting off east.

Still grinning, Tranter rose from the protection of the rocks. Elation ran a scintillating course through him. 'Well, that should bring that sonofabitch McAdam runnin',' he said. 'You ready for him, boys?'

Complacent smiles were his reward. 'You betcha, boss,' said one, slapping his holstered Colt. 'That old man has been lucky too long.'

Tranter grinned happily. 'Exactly my sentiments, boys,' he said. 'Now, I reckon it's bedtime. Figure we got time for that.

McAdam, if nothin' else, bein' a cautious man, will weigh up the odds before he comes a knockin'.'

Gleeful guffaws greeted his comment.

'But just before we go,' Tranter went on, 'guess we should see if the rock fence we've just constructed across the canyon has cut McAdam off from his water. Surprisin' what these acts of nature can do,' he opined with a smug grin. 'I reckon that's what it was, don't you, boys? An act of nature. Rock faces do sheer with erosion and frosts and the like. Too bad fer McAdam, I guess. It'll kinda make that part of his range mine from now on, more than likely.'

More raucous laughter greeted his remarks. They swaggered to the now shattered rim of the chasm. Lined along the edge they peered into the dark abyss. The westering moonshine did not light up their night's work—the slanting rays throwing too deep a shadow, and the still rising dust didn't help, either. But they faintly saw the huge pile of rock and it looked good.

Tranter felt a warm happiness glow through him. The job *must* be done, he decided. They had set enough explosive to blow up Hell.

'Come-on, boys,' he said. 'I don't think we need worry about gittin' to water on the south range any longer. McAdam's got that worry, now—on his *north* range.'

More guffaws filled the night.

'But, boys, there's just one other thing ...' Tranter gazed across the pleased faces of his crew. 'I got to leave a welcomin' party. Harry, you up to it?'

Harry Barras, late of rustling sprees on the Mexico–Texas border before the Rangers had ambushed their outfit, grinned. But he often recalled he had been lucky to get out of that fracas with his life. Like a badge, and as was the custom down there, he still wore his Colt in the cross-draw position with pride. He pawed the butt. 'Be good to get into action again,' he said.

'Nothin' fancy,' said Tranter smoothly, still bathing in the afterglow of this apparently successful venture, 'just organize a welcoming party, maybe draw a little blood, then you can make for home.'

Barras grinned once more. He patted the Spencer carbine nestled in the scabbard lashed to his saddle. 'Ol' Betsy's lead'll make a real mess of a man, if he's hit right.'

'Then do it,' said Tranter, 'but don't end up like Harkness an' Collins, fer God's sake.'

Barras's deep-tanned, swarthy face lit up, his blue eyes glittered. 'You're sendin' a man to do a man's job this time. There'll be a ruckus made, you bet.'

'Yeah ...?' Tranter couldn't disguise the doubt he felt. But he continued, 'Then—like I said—get out. I want all my boys around the spread when the news of this breaks.' He stared around him. 'We know nothin', heard nothin', seen nothin', right?'

The booming explosion slamming across the night brought Taw McAdam slowly out of his deep sleep. Still drowsy and trying to analyse what had awakened him he listened to the last of its roar before it tailed off into rolling silence across the range. Then, breaking through into his still sleep-drugged awareness, he heard the clatter of boots down the passage, heard a door bang. That had to be Pa, he thought.

Fully awake now he rolled out of bed. Still in his range garb, the need to dress didn't arise. He bounded to the door, opened it and went down the passage. Soon he was out on to the bare ground before the ranch-house.

He saw his father standing bare-headed, his long, white and black streaked locks stark in the moonlight. He was bellowing, 'What in the name of Jesus was that, Marty?'

Taw could see Marty Graham was

coming up from the shadows of the barn. 'Came from Ellis Canyon, Mr McAdam. Lay big odds on that. I reckon it's got to be dynamite.'

'An' it's got to be Tranter!' exploded Brad McAdam. 'Why, that low-down ...'

Taw came to his side, his mind in confusion, still a little sleep-sluggish. 'What we goin' to do, Pa?' he fumbled. 'Go after him?'

Taw could see his father was shaking with anger. 'That's just what ...'

Brad McAdam paused. Taw met his fierce stare. It was soon clear to Taw his father was now fighting desperately to calm himself down. Finally he said, 'That's just what he wants us to do, son. So we don't. We go see what damage there is first. Then we speak with the Cross family and plan.'

While his father talked, light had come on in the bunkhouse. It emptied of hands fast. They were now standing in different states of dress on the hard-packed ground in front of the ranch-house staring at Brad McAdam, bemused, silent questions written on their startled faces. Flora McAdam now came out on to the stoop. Her hair had rags tied in it, to maintain its curl, Taw knew. But she stood quietly. This was men's work. She would only comment if asked. Behind her was *her* domain, which she ruled firmly and was greatly respected there.

Brad McAdam stared around him and growled, 'Well, get saddled, men. We go see what damage there is.'

When they reached the wide opening of Ellis Canyon, the dawn sun's rays were gilding the range. Long before they got to the canyon's narrows, in the burgeoning sunlight, they could see the bright, red-ochre scar on the rimrock where the stone had been blasted off.

Taw watched the stern lines on his pa's features deepen. For most of the ride Brad McAdam had kept preening his long, sagging moustache, blinking lids over hard grey eyes, and had been silent. What he was thinking was anybody's guess; certainly Taw wouldn't hazard one. But though his pa looked raw with anger and his mood made taciturn by it, he seemed in control of his emotions. Taw had seldom seen this side of his father. Pa was usually an amiable, generous, kindly man in a restrained way. But, he knew, when the need arose there was a core of iron right through him.

As they rode, the canyon walls pinched in ever narrower. Each side of the stream that flowed towards them was chewed by the hooves of many cattle making for water over the years. Finally they reached the rock fall, but before they had got fully up to it, Taw heard a chuckle begin deep down inside his pa. When his father turned in the saddle, his face was lit up with delight. 'The sonofabitch has failed,' he crowed. 'Tranter's plan's fallen flat on its face!'

Whooping with joy, he urged his horse

into a long stride, towards where the rock had failed to close the canyon and cut off the access to water.

Seeing his father's reckless run, alarm coursed through Taw. 'Pa, hold it!' he yelled. 'Could be guns on the rimrock!'

Even as he said it, a rifle cracked, rampaging noise down the canyon and Taw's heart jumped up into his throat as he saw his father topple out of the saddle.

THIRTEEN

By his pocket watch it was two in the morning when Simpson moved into the draw he had ridden up to escape the posse that morning. Entering it told him his ride through Midanbar Canyon had ended and he was back in the basin again. It had been an eerie ride in the full moonlight, the tall spires of rock seeming to take on an almost grotesque human form that occasionally sent prickles up his backbone. He also had the feeling that he was being followed, but it was only a feeling. The occasions he had looked back, he had seen nothing, even though it was bright moonlight and he could see a considerable distance.

Out of the draw he watered his horse and himself at the stream there, then turned the grey along the ridge and headed for the high Pecon Hills and the trail to the M-M.

It was as he was coming out of the tailings of the hills and on to the level range that the night was shattered by the huge explosion. It came roaring across the range at him from the north. He saw the flash in the far distance.

Moments later he observed small blobs of light blossom where he knew the M-M buildings to be. What, in the name of ...? He set his chin. He began to accept it took little imagination to figure he'd ridden into this basin when things had been on the verge of popping into wide open hostility, due, it appeared from all he had heard and observed, to Tranter's pure, naked ambition and ruthless aggression.

Simpson spat. Well, he was in it as deep as he could be. He didn't like it, but there it was. He'd stay, see it through. If nothing else, he owed his horse that. And he was also cultivating a powerful curiosity as to why Tranter seemed to want his hide so much. It was plain unnatural. He'd have thought his going out of the basin would have given Tranter one thing less to bother about and should have allowed him to depart unimpeded.

When he rode into the M-M yard twenty minutes later, there were lights still on in the ranch-house. The front door was ajar. Then Flora McAdam stepped out on to the stoop. She had a Winchester held ready to fire. She lowered it.

'Mr Simpson,' she said. She sounded surprised.

Simpson climbed down wearily and touched his hat. 'Ma'am. You seem to be havin' trouble.'

'There was an explosion in Ellis Canyon,' she said. 'Brad, Taw and the boys have gone to see what it was all about.'

'Sounded like dynamite to me, ma'am.' Simpson narrowed his eyelids. 'That the place where there is a dispute over who owns the water?'

'Yes.' Mrs McAdam nodded her head

firmly. 'But there's no dispute, only of Bart Tranter's making. It's ours by legal right.' Then Mrs McAdam waved the Winchester. A frown creased her brow. 'You're riding a different horse ...'

'I met with some trouble, ma'am,' Simpson said. 'Kind of trouble that seems to be comin' your way, too.'

'Tranter?'

'I think so. Plus a posse from Hell, wantin' to arrest me for the shootin' of Abel Cross and his men.'

Flora McAdam looked indignant. 'Why, that has got to be wrong.'

'I'm glad to say Marshal Patter seems to think so, too, but some of his posse don't. So until Taw can stand as a witness, I guess I'll be on the run an' tryin' to find out who really did it, if only to clear my name.'

'Well, I have coffee on the hot plate inside,' Mrs McAdam said. 'Come in. You look as though you could use some.'

Simpson allowed his body to relax. He

felt immensely tired. 'Won't argue with that, ma'am,' he admitted. 'Then I got a favour to ask you, seein' as Brad ain't around. I need a fresh horse. Want to go after your menfolk. There could maybe be some evidence to help us find some answers up there.'

Flora McAdam looked thoughtfully at him for moments. 'I'm thinking you may be right, Mr Simpson,' she said.

Then, more out of curiosity than anything else, Simpson said, 'Did Taw see the Cross folk?'

Flora McAdam seemed uncertain. 'I think so. He came home late. I haven't had the opportunity to speak with him.'

'I see.' Simpson followed Mrs McAdam into the house.

Simpson, now full of coffee, ham and eggs watched dawn crack the eastern horizon as he headed out for Ellis Canyon on a sturdy sorrel loaned by the M-M. Flora McAdam's soft-spoken directions were still gentle on his ear as he crossed the range.

The five cups of coffee he'd had had revived him, but the strain of being without sleep for two nights was still heavy on him. He loped across the grama grass towards the canyon. He soon realized it ran almost parallel to Midanbar Canyon and he began to scan the range anxiously as the light increased. He figured Patter and his posse could still be hacking around in the Midanbar, or searching Bart Tranter's range, but Hewson ... that was another matter entirely. By now, he felt sure, that coyote could be on his back trail.

The faint crack of a firearm ahead caused him to ease up on the sorrel before he pressed on with more urgency. Rifle fire for sure. Soon the maw of Ellis Canyon began to show. A stream came out of it, lined with cottonwoods. It was entirely different to the Midanbar, being only three hundred yards across and narrowing the more he rode up it. The stream flowed sluggishly along the only slightly sloping bottom.

Then beyond the bend ahead he heard the urgent thump of horses' hooves coming towards him. He'd only time to rein up, pull and line up his Winchester. He lowered it when he saw Brad McAdam gallop round the corner slumped in the saddle and three of his riders siding him. Simpson could also see blood on the rancher's shirt, see the wound had been crudely padded and wrapped.

'McAdam!' he said, then demanded, 'What's happened?'

McAdam looked relieved it wasn't more danger. 'I think it's Tranter. Blown the canyon rim. Attempted to block it off, stop me gettin' to my own water's my guess. Left a man on the rimrock with a long gun. He hit me. Taw went after him before I could stop him.'

There was no time for a lot of discussion, Simpson decided. He needed to go after Taw. Though enthusiastic, the boy was still raw. And there could be answers if they caught up with that sonofabitch bushwhacker. He declared his intention, finishing with, 'You go get yourself fixed up, McAdam.' Then he narrowed his stare. 'You reckon the wound is serious?'

McAdam pursed thin lips, his face grey. Pain was in his eyes. 'More messy than serious, I reckon, but it needs tendin' to.'

'How far up the canyon?' prompted Simpson then.

'Mebbe a half mile,' McAdam gasped. 'Watch yourself, Simpson. An' try an' watch out fer my boy.'

Simpson kneed the sorrel forward. 'I'll do my best on both counts,' he called over his shoulder.

He soon came to the blasted rimrock and urged the sorrel past it, skirting the large pool he found on the other side. All the time he rode he scanned the edge of the canyon. Then he heard the roar of guns ahead. It had to be Taw.

Simpson found there was a drift of aspen and fir a mile on past the water where the canyon began to open out again before it flattened into open range country once more. He could see the blue-white plumes of gunsmoke drifting amongst the tree boles. There was also a dead horse about a hundred yards from the timber. Then, to Simpson's cautious relief, he saw Taw's pinto tied up a couple of hundred yards away, east side of the area of the gun battle.

Deeper in the trees, a further crackle of gunfire ripped the early morning. Simpson scanned the situation. If he got around the back of the trees, he could maybe cut off any retreat from there.

He urged his horse into a run, taking a wide turn around the timber stand. Three hundred yards on it thinned out into grass again. And still the gunfire snapped, a hard sound. There was quite a shindig going on in there.

In a rash of rocks Simpson climbed down, unsheathed his Winchester and waited. After five minutes of hot, noisy conflict a man came running out of the trees. Taw loped out on long legs fifty yards behind, then stopped and raised his rifle and roared, 'Drop your weapon, you sonofabitch, or I'll kill you.'

Harry Barras swung around. He gaped. Just a wet-eared kid, God damn it! His wasted face was twisted with rage. 'Go to hell,' he snarled and brought up his long gun.

Taw triggered his Spencer. His lead slapped Barras back, arms wide, his own Spencer carbine flying out of his hand. He hit the ground hard and lay writhing and moaning.

'I told you to drop your damned gun, why didn't you?' raged Taw. To Simpson, the boy now sounded shaken as well as angry. However Taw began to move forward while jacking in another load.

Simpson came out from the rocks. 'Taw,' he urged, 'approach him careful.'

Young McAdam lifted his startled gaze,

began to swing up the rifle again before he lowered when he recognized him. 'Carl! Hell, how did you git here? Ain't you headed out?'

Simpson said, 'Long story.'

Taw waved his rifle, as if in anger, at the wounded bushwhacker. 'I told him to drop the damned gun. Damn it, why did he make me shoot? Ain't ever shot a man before.'

Simpson felt a brief flush of sympathy for Taw flood through him. He knew the feelings now churning in the boy. He'd known those self same feelings himself one time. It never came easy to kill a man, or wound him if you weren't cut out for it, though it got easier with time and necessity.

Then he saw Barras was raising the Colt. 'Move, Taw,' he bellowed and fired his rifle from the hip as the boy went sideways and dropped to the ground.

Barras's Colt roared, but the shot went high as Simpson's lead hit him full in the brisket, smacking him back to the grass once more.

'Jesus, hell,' growled Taw, scrambling to his feet, 'don't they ever give up? I thought I'd git him when I downed his horse, but he ran for the trees still smokin' his damn gun.'

'The hard ones don't,' said Simpson. 'But you were right to give him the chance.'

Taw raised his left hand, the one without a weapon in it, and stared at it. Simpson could see it was shaking badly. Wide-eyed Taw said, 'God awmighty, will you look at that?'

'It'll pass,' said Simpson.

He went to Barras. To his surprise, the sonofabitch was still alive, but only just. 'Mister, who you workin' for?' he rasped.

Taw cut in, 'I can tell you that ... Tranter.'

Barras coughed, managed a grin that was more a grimace as he stared up at them. Blood trickled down his whiskers from the corner of his mouth. Simpson met his gaze.

'The boy's good,' he said.

'You know anythin' about the Cross killings?' demanded Simpson.

The Texas brushpopper stared up with china blue eyes, bubbled a laugh. 'We sure nailed them good, huh?' Then he frowned. 'Jees, maybe I shouldn't have said that. Shit.'

He coughed again, then his eyes rolled up and his head flopped to one side. Simpson knew the bushwhacker would never again utter another word, or see another sunset.

He rose from kneeling beside Barras. He stared at Taw. 'You hear what he said, Taw, about the Cross shootin's?'

Taw's face was pale grey through his tan. He passed a still shaking hand across his mouth. 'By God, sure I heard it. Tranter kilt 'em? But why?'

'I'd say he just wants more an' he's in

such a hurry he don't give a damn how he gets it. How long did you say he's been in this basin?'

'Not much more than a year.'

'Sonofabitch,' said Simpson. 'Where did he come from?'

Taw shrugged. 'Nobody knows for sure. Just bought the place off Jack Slaughter an' moved in. Got rid of most of the crew an' imported his own men. Soon after, things began happenin' on the range. Nathan Mather got bushwhacked. Hoss Dakin burnt out on the Boney River. Tranter bought him out 'cos Hoss couldn't afford to rebuild, bin worryin' at Widow Mather to do likewise an' gittin' Pa real mad by contestin' the water rights here in Ellis Canyon. Got to be him that blew that caprock.'

Then Taw stared aghast as Simpson went backwards, red spurting from the side of his head, his slouch hat flying off. Simultaneously, the boom of a big rifle thundered across the meadow they were on. Taw stared as Simpson hit the ground hard.

Taw found himself momentarily transfixed as he watched the blood stream from Carl's wound. Then Taw realized his knees felt as though they were turning to water. Panic grasped him. He must get into cover, or he'd finish up the same as Carl! He turned and ran, pounding ground for the trees, making for his pinto on the other side of them. After that. God, after that?

FOURTEEN

In his hiding place in the rocks Coke Hewson lowered his big Sharps rifle and smiled bleakly as he saw Simpson hit the ground. Then he saw young Taw McAdam run for the trees. It surprised him, for he knew the boy was a hothead. He'd expected him to start blazing away with that Spencer he had to prove he was a man. Nice to see a boy show good sense. He, for sure, didn't want to kill him. There were no dollars in that ... yet.

He stowed the rifle, proud of the fact that he had guessed right this time and had picked up Simpson's tracks in the canyon. And he'd felt sure Simpson had sensed somebody was on his back trail, for he'd kept looking back. So Simpson had been a damned fool not to be more cautious. Hewson narrowed mean eyes, felt superior. When Simpson had ridden on into the M-M confines he'd waited, then trailed him when he'd come out again and headed for Ellis Canyon on that fresh sorrel.

Hewson had found himself curious about that one, too, when he'd heard the boom of the dynamite in the night. At the recollection, Hewson's knife-scarred lips twitched into the pretence of a smile. Had to be Tranter. Sure as hell, like a man possessed, that sonofabitch wanted to be the man around here and was in a big hurry to establish that fact. Maybe the smart man thought if he moved fast enough the less questions there would be to answer, if enough palms were greased. Either way, it was very likely the overall situation developing around here would earn Coke Hewson a lot of dollars before it was through.

Satisfied with that, Hewson stowed his big rifle into the saddle boot he'd had especially made to take it. The Sharps was the best rifle he had ever had—for all types of game. Then he climbed up on to the back of his horse and cantered over to where Simpson lay on the grama grass.

He looked down. Blood covered the whole of the left-hand side of Simpson's face. It was a mess. The job looked to be done, nevertheless Hewson drew his Colt. He had to make sure.

But riding his pinto and coming to the edge of the trees and seeing Hewson's deadly move nearly stopped Taw Mc-Adam's heart. He'd forced himself to come back. He felt shame now that he had panicked. But he'd just wanted to get to his horse, felt he had to, felt it might be the best course to take. He hadn't known what to do after that. He'd just found this disgust for himself and the urge welling up in him to return and get Carl to safety, choose what it cost him.

But at the distance he was he couldn't quite make out who it was looking down at

Carl; however there was something familiar about him and a name would come, he felt sure. Another thing, he had no time at the moment to speculate.

He hoisted his Spencer. Three hundred yards, he estimated. He didn't expect to hit anything from this distance, but he had to do something quick—frighten the bastard off shooting Carl again if nothing else. If there was any hope at all that Carl was alive, he had to do that.

The Spencer's flat noise smacked ringing echoes across the range. The ambusher looked up, startled, forgetting what he was about. Taw fired again, anxiously. He'd temporarily forgotten all Pa had taught him. That was take his time and make sure. But it wasn't as easy as that when your buddy was on the ground helpless, and a man was about to shoot him.

Even so, Taw felt a certain anxiety as the bushwhacker brought up that big rifle and lined it up on him. He swung the pinto and tried to make for the trees once more and cover, but the boom of the rifle and his horse screaming and collapsing under him put a stop to that.

Taw went over its head and hit the ground hard. The impact jarred every bone in his body, sent the wind "hoofing" out of him. Dazed he tried to collect his wits as he scrambled up, but he still clutched his rifle.

When he'd gathered his senses sufficiently, he saw the big bushwhacking bastard was lining up his Colt again on Carl. This time, one thing Taw was sure of: he was getting a picture of who he was firing at now. He was certain it was that damned hunter who lived in the Pecons, Coke Hewson—or he'd eat his hat for supper.

In desperation, Taw upped the Spencer and fired once more. He saw Hewson's horse jump and squeal and start to run across the range. Feeling immense relief and glee, Taw saw Hewson was hanging on and cursing aplenty, fighting hard to hold the animal. Triumph surged through Taw. He must have creased the big roan and it was running to hell and gone, too sore and scared to heed Hewson's vicious attempts to check it.

But Taw also realized it wouldn't last long. He stared around him anxiously. He could see the sorrel Carl had been riding was now calmly standing head down and cropping grass nearby. That horse had to be his only chance. On high boots he ran with awkward steps towards the animal. He could see it was one of the ranch horses. Grasping the reins he swung up. He headed back to Carl.

Reaching him, Taw stared at the terrible injury. God, Carl's head appeared to have had its left side torn away. It was that damned brute of a gun Hewson had. Taw knew those big Sharps rifles could wreak terrible damage. Carl must be near to death. Must be.

He didn't know whether it was his fear

of Hewson, or fear for Carl's safety that put sufficient strength in him to allow him to lift Carl's dead-weight, unconscious body and drape him over the sorrel's withers. But whichever it was he did it with alacrity.

With the hairs bristling up on the back of his neck as he expected the boom of Hewson's big rifle to crash out again and himself feeling the pounding of Hewson's lead smacking into his back, he went up into the saddle behind Carl. He turned the animal, which was skittish about having the smell of Carl's blood in its nostrils, and lashed its rump.

'Git on!' he bellowed. 'Git on!'

He ran the sorrel at a flat out gallop, not sparing it. Soon it was blowing and sweat foam and saliva spewed back from its jaws. Taw ignored it as it splashed on to him. Soon a lather of sweat covered the beast, but still it ran gamely, its head bobbing, its mane flying.

Taw headed for home, the undulating

grama grass speeding by under him. All the time he expected that fatal bullet to crash into him. He lashed the sorrel some more. Fifteen minutes later he could almost feel the tension drain out of him as he ran over a swell of land and saw the M-M buildings in the distance.

He drew his Colt and fired off two shots. Their booming echoes snapped flatly across the range as he urged the sorrel on. Now he saw two dark specks with trains of dust flying up behind them come out from the ranch towards him. He only eased up when the two riders met him. To his surprise he saw they were Clute Cross and Marshal Patter.

He pulled down the sorrel to a walk. It was about spent. It was snorting and blowing, its flanks heaving, but it still had something left. Taw right away figured it a good replacement for his own horse—the one he'd had to shoot, back in the desert.

'What's the commotion?' asked Patter, pulling rein. Then his narrow gaze found

Carl's body. 'By God, Hewson got to him, huh?'

Not knowing how Patter had managed to deduce that, Taw nodded. 'Was him all right. Got to get Carl to the ranch, Marshal, an' Ma. She'll know what to do, if there's any hope at all.'

Patter's face grew grave as he stared at Simpson's vivid, cruel wound. 'Yup. Guess it's that bad, by the look of it.'

Without answering, Taw urged his horse on towards the ranch. The two riders fell in beside him.

As they rode Patter continued earnestly, as if he wanted to reassure Taw, 'But I've found a lotta wounds can look bad but ain't when it comes down to it.'

Not comforted, Taw sent the sorrel into a canter. Patter and Clute stepped up the pace with him.

Now Patter said, his face grim, 'But right now, as marshal of Hell, I gotta ask, boy. You break Simpson out t'other night?'

Taw glared, amazed at such single-minded lawman thinking. 'You reckon this is the time an' place fer that?'

Patter's gaze was serious, almost severe. 'I got a sound reason, boy. I want to know if Simpson, an' yourself for that matter, are innocent of Abel Cross's, Jimmy Sands' and Lew Beel's deaths.'

Taw screwed up his bruised face. He said fiercely, 'Well, I tell you now, Marshal, that weren't nothin' to do with us. But me an' Carl here sure as hell know who *did* do it.' As he continued to push his mount hard he told of Harry Barras's confession.

Patter stared as he rose and fell in the saddle with the motion of the horse. 'An' Barras is dead?'

'It was him or me, Marshal,' Taw snorted, 'though Carl here hit him with the killin' bullet. If he hadn't have done you'd have found the both of *us* more than likely laying dead back there.'

Patter pursed his lips, raised bushy

brows. 'Well, it don't surprise me about Barras. I got a dodger on him on'y t'other day. Three hundred dollars' reward. Guess you've saved the county a job. Now, about Hewson ...'

Taw snorted, 'If I hadn't nicked his hoss, sent it runnin', he'd have got me, too.'

Patter's brown gaze turned hard. 'So, how was it done?' he quizzed. 'Did he stop you on the trail?'

Taw told what had happened. When he finished, Patter shook his head. 'God damn. A straight bushwhackin'? No warnin'? Though it shouldn't surprise me. Well, you showed grit, boy, takin' on the likes of him, but you shouldn't have gone back.'

Bobbing anxiously in the saddle, holding Simpson with one hand, Taw stared. 'Hell, I wasn't about to watch him spread Carl's brains all over the range.'

By now they'd got to the M-M confines. They dismounted. Flora McAdam came off the stoop she'd been standing on, shading her eyes, watching them come in. Her face was lined with concern. 'Is that Mr Simpson?'

Taw began to carry Carl into the big living room of the ranch-house. 'Been hit bad, Ma,' he said as he walked, then stared amazed at the roomful of those whom he knew to be some of the townspeople of Hell—traders and the like—stained with trail dust and fast asleep on the floor or on pieces of furniture, their vibrating snores loud.

Stopping in his tracks he said, 'What the h ...' then remembered his father's rule on no bad language in his mother's presence and waited for her to answer.

'Marshal Patter's posse,' she said. 'All you need to know for now. Now take Mr Simpson through to the kitchen table,' she ordered, calmly but firmly. 'I'll see what the damage is. Doctor Crowley, the physician in Hell, has already been sent for to tend to your father.'

Feeling instant anxiety Taw said, 'Pa OK?'

'If there's no infection, he'll live,' said Flora McAdam, but Taw saw her lips tighten, her pale face grow concerned, though she quickly masked it. 'Now move on.'

In the kitchen she busily cleared the big, rough-hewn deal table of crockery. 'Lay him on that, son,' she said.

He was amazed by her calmness, until he remembered his ma had been a field nurse during the North–South conflict and must have seen much worse than this. Taw watched her bend over the unconscious Carl and inspect the wound. Then she got water and bathed it. 'Lucky,' she said. 'Seems to have entered along the temple,' she explained while she worked, 'curved around the skull and come out at the back of his head. Tore a flap of skin there. He'll have a terrible headache when he wakes up and a lot of bruising.'

She busily began to dress it with fresh

bandages made from the remains of the sheet she had torn up previously to pad and wrap her husband's chest wound.

As she worked, a commotion started outside. Anxious and curious, Taw went out on to the stoop. He was amazed to see Coke Hewson riding in from the north range.

Marshal Patter was already outside, standing with Clute Cross. 'The damned gall of the man,' the marshal growled as Taw joined him.

Hewson rode in close and reined up. Taw could see the bloody bullet burn on the horse's rump. Big and menacing in the saddle Hewson stared down. 'You got Simpson?' he said.

Taw stepped forward, hand moving for his Colt. 'Why, you sonofabitch, you know damn well ...'

Marshal Patter's hand restrained him. 'Hold it, boy,' he said. He looked up at Hewson. 'Taw here said you shot Simpson from ambush. That right?'

Hewson looked surprised but his black stare was mocking. 'Christ, that what the boy told you?'

Patter nodded. 'That's what he said.'

'Well he's lyin',' Hewson said blandly. 'I stopped them on the trail, after they'd killed Harry Barras. He tell you about that? I told Simpson I was takin' him in. He went for his Colt. Taw here turned and ran.'

Taw felt rage rush through him. 'You Goddamned liar ...'

Taw felt the pressure of the marshal's hand on his arm again. 'Leave it to me, boy,' he said, and turned to the hunter. 'Hewson, I've heard another story.'

'It ain't the right one,' said the hunter. Then added impatiently, 'Now, all I want to know is, is Simpson dead?'

Rage erupting into his throat Taw roared, 'You goin' to believe him, Marshal? Goddamn it, he shot Carl from ambush. That's God's honest truth.'

Patter rested hipshot, his right hand

now moving to his hip, near his Colt. 'Knowin' Hewson here, I'm inclined to believe you, Taw,' he droned evenly. 'But I can't work on gut feelin's. My lawman trainin' requires me to be certain.'

With that bald statement Hewson's face darkened with rage. He barked, 'You callin' me a liar agin that hell-raisin' boy? Well, to hell with this. I'm askin' you if Simpson's dead. I got two hundred dollars' bounty money comin' if he is, put there by a representative of the people of Hell—as well you know, Patter.'

Surprising Taw, Marshal Patter laughed, but it was without humour. It was more in contempt. 'You got nothin' comin', Hewson,' he said. 'Simpson's still alive, thank God. An' we have proof it was Tranter's men who shot Cross and his hands so you almost killed an innocent man. I warned not to try it. Now you're wanted for attempted murder.'

It was then Patter went for his Colt.

But Hewson appeared ready for it. He

snarled. His right hand blurred. His Colt came up within the blinking of an eye. It stilled every man's hand, frozen claw-like over their own weapons.

Hewson laughed harshly. 'You'll have to get up earlier than that to fool me, Patter. You telegraphed that draw. God, it's a miracle you're still alive, the trade you're in. As for attempted murder, I was carryin' out the wishes of Saul Pollard, a duly elected member of Hell's council, actin' on their behalf when he put the bounty on Simpson. You heard him yourself. So forget any ideas about takin' me in. In attemptin' to arrest Simpson, I was doin' my bounden duty as a citizen of this basin an' ignorant of later alleged evidence.' That mouthful put the hunter in a different category, thought Patter. It would easily influence a jury. Hewson had been educated at one time for sure.

He watched the hunter begin to back off the big roan he was riding. And Patter thought, he has the sense not to shoot here, too. Beside him, Taw growled in frustration, stepped forward. Again, Patter restrained him. 'Don't be a damned fool, boy,' he said. 'Pollard did put money on Simpson's head. An' Hewson didn't know of Barras's confession. He would get away with it easily in any court of law. It'll keep. We'll git him.'

But Taw wasn't so sure and stared angrily as Hewson cantered off, his big frame erect and menacing atop his roan.

FIFTEEN

Along with Marshal Patter and Clute Cross, Taw watched Coke Hewson ride off towards Ellis Canyon. Taw's rage was solid. How could a man get away with it, as easy as that?

Marshal Patter rubbed his chin thoughtfully. 'Goin' on gut feelin',' he said, 'I reckon he's made some deal with Bart Tranter when he took Montana Collins back to the Boxed T.'

'Collins?' said Taw. 'What happened to him?'

Patter's gaze turned. 'Course, you don't know. Tried to bushwhack your friend Simpson, out there in the Pecons. That's why Simpson's here now instead of maybe in Grand Creek, t'other side of those hills.' Patter's grey look was steady. He went on to describe finding Carl—then the chase through the Midanbar Canyon ... all he knew, in fact. Told how he and the posse finished up here at the M-M two hours ago after riding all night, back tracking Carl and Hewson's trails. He had wanted to go on, he explained, but the possemen were spent. He said you couldn't expect semi-sedentary men to last as long as hardened saddlemen in bad country, but added he was proud they'd stuck to the trail as long as they had. He and Clute had just been starting out again when they heard his, Taw's, shots and saw him coming over the hill.

Taw said then, 'So what now, Marshal? Ain't we goin' after Hewson? An' why is Tranter so keen on gittin' Carl? Got to be he sent Montana Collins to bushwhack him.'

Patter raised his brows, rubbed his strong jaw thoughtfully. 'That's what's beginning to trouble me, too, boy. There's a whole lot about this business we gotta find out.'

'You goin' out to the Boxed T, Marshal?' demanded Clute Cross, for the first time really joining in the conversation. He'd always been on the taciturn side had Clute, Taw knew, but friendly. Clute went on. 'Taw said Barras had confessed that it was Tranter an' his men shot down Pa, Beel an' Jimmy Sands.'

'It's evidence from a dead man, Clute,' said Patter. 'We'll have a time provin' it, takin' into consideration the type of law Tranter could get to back him up. An' to enforce an arrest we'll have to go out there to the Boxed T in force. I think we should get the M-M and the Circle C to pool their hands, get men from the county, too, to give us a real chance of obtaining an arrest. Tranter has some hard men up there. An' he ain't done anythin' we can prove, 'less we can get somebody to accept the possibility of clemency an' spill the beans.'

'Nothin' we can prove!' snorted Taw irately. 'Damn it, he blew Ellis Canyon ...'

'You don't know that,' said Patter.

225

'How come it was Harry Barras waitin' on the rimrock when we rode up an' shot Pa, if it weren't Tranter?' Taw declared.

Patter raised thick brows. 'Yup, I go along with your suspicions, but it's not proof. Tranter could say he put him there to guard his borders, things the way they are.'

Taw glowered. 'Whose damned side are you on?' he snorted. Then, relenting, said, 'Well, failin' that, would a dyin' man lie about Tranter shootin' Clute's pa an' his two hands, if it weren't so?'

Patter's gaze was steady. 'I guess not but it's just your word he did confess,' he pointed out. '*I* believe you, Taw—knowing you an' watchin' you grow up fer ten years—but Tranter's lawyers would chew you up an' spit you out if you tried that without Barras there to back you up, don't you see that?'

'Well, to hell with lawyers!' raged Taw.

Patter sighed wearily. 'Yup, well, sometimes I'm inclined to think that way myself, Taw. So, like I say, best thing we can do is organize a posse big enough an' bring Tranter in on suspicion. Then we can work on his men for a confession.'

Clute said, fervently, 'Pa would've said to hell with that.'

Patter nodded. 'Truth be known, one time, so would I. But times they are a'changin', boys. So we do it my way. Clute, ride to the Circle C, bring your men in to here soon as you can. I'll return to town, send a wire to Sheriff Tom Boot in Serela. Taw, you stay put until I say otherwise, y'hear? Don't do anythin' stupid.'

Taw growled. 'All o' this is goin' to take a coon's age,' he protested.

'It's goin' to be done right,' instructed Patter. 'Tranter's goin' nowhere, or his men. My guess is he'll be sittin' tight fer a spell, actin' innocent, or maybe he's hopin' the M-M'll go chargin' up there an' start blazin' away, givin' him a legitimate reason to get rid of them, if that's what he aims to do.'

Clute Cross said grudgingly, 'Well, you're the law, Marshal, but I go along with Taw. Still, I guess Ma'll play it your way when I tell her.'

Patter said. 'The wisdom of age, Clute.' He turned. 'Taw?'

The young McAdam shuffled. 'Pa said we should wait,' he admitted. 'Go in together with the Circle C.'

Patter appeared content he'd won them round. 'A sensible man. Right, boys. Maybe this time tomorrow, things'll be beginnin' to move in our favour.'

When Simpson came round he took minutes to orientate himself. He found himself in a room, wrapped in blankets and lying on an iron frame bed. Through the small window he saw it was dark outside, but the big moon was up stranding silver through the aperture. His head felt as though it was exploding. He groaned and reared up. That caused more pain to savage him. Gingerly, he felt at the bandage Doc Crowley had wound around his head hours earlier. How he had got here was momentarily confusing him, but he figured it was the M-M ranch-house he lay in. Now he remembered snatches of what had happened before it all went black. It had been daylight ... the shootout with Barras ... the confession Barras had made before he died about the Cross killings ... riding with Taw, then nothing.

It didn't take much to deduce he'd been shot, how badly he could only guess at, but the left-hand side of his face was a mass of snarling pain hammering across his head. And there could only be one prime suspect for the shooting ... Coke Hewson.

Cold rage at the thought of that sonofabitch caused Simpson to throw off his sheets and stand up. Agony and nausea hit him even more severely. Gasping, he leaned on the wall for support. The throb in his head increased, causing him to breathe rapidly as it drummed across his temples. He stood there for moments, gathering himself, trying to dominate his pain and all the time felt the need for violent revenge growing inside him. A couple of days ago he'd been a peaceable man, riding a peaceable trail. He could blame Taw. He didn't. He could blame Tranter. He did. For some reason that sonofabitch seemed to want him dead. Now he had to know why. As for Hewson come the hour there would be accounts to call in.

He saw his clothes, washed and placed in a neat pile on a chair near the bed. Mrs McAdam? He dressed quickly, fighting the pain that was threatening to overwhelm him again. His head still pounded, but the sick feeling was clearing slowly.

Now, in the light of the moon coming through the window he saw his gun rig hanging on the bed-head rail. He strapped it on, feeling the comfort of its weight at his hip. He moved to the door, paused to recover as more waves of nausea hit him, then went out into the dark passageway.

The occupants of the house were asleep. He could hear their slumbering noises. He should wake somebody, find out a few things, but he had this burning inside him to reach Tranter, reach Hewson, move in a straight line like he had done in the Con Valley war when the chips had been really down. He might get arguments against straight-line confrontation if he suggested it here. Patter was cautious to a degree, so was Brad McAdam. Taw was too young to be involved. Yes, he had to handle this himself. Head right for trouble now. Confront it and deal with it. They wouldn't be expecting him. He would have to ride to the Boxed T. North they had said, through Ellis Canyon.

He padded into the large common room and out through the door into the moonlight. Outside, there was a welcome pail hanging, a ladle hung with it. He took a long drink, then realized how hungry he was. He went back into the house and looked for food in the kitchen. The act of gnawing the cold beef he found in the fly-proof free-standing larder caused pain to once more pound through his scraped and bruised head. Trying to ignore it he moved out into the night. He was quietly pleased to find his saddle trappings and rifle in the tack room.

But preoccupied with his nausea and his throbbing head, which was causing him to shamble about, he was surprised he hadn't woken somebody. Logic said they must be sleeping light, things the way they were. However, he seemed to be getting away with it. He carried his gear and moved to the door of the tack room, then paused. Across the bare ground he saw the bunkhouse door open. He withdrew, back into the shadows. He watched a hand go to the john, return, heard and saw the door bang to. All went silent again, except for a coyote calling out in the basin.

With renewed caution he selected a horse from the remuda and saddled up.

Continuing to fight the nausea caused by the pounding pain in the side of his head he climbed up and rode out into the moon-silvered night. Though it hurt like hell to stare up at the canopy of stars overhead, he established his bearings from them quickly and he headed for Ellis Canyon and the Boxed T.

Too late, Flora McAdam watched Carl Simpson head into the night. Something had woken her. She had gone to the bedroom window to admire the beauty of the night. Behind her, her husband slept uneasily in the bed she had just left, propped up, his chest wound bound tightly. She could see sweat sheened his forehead.

But what was Mr Simpson doing? She felt concern rush through her. He should be kept in bed for at least a week. He must be suffering untold discomfort, severe pain in fact, moving about like that. Perhaps he was attempting to leave the basin without hindrance this time, no matter what discomfort it caused him. But she sensed intuitively that that would not be Carl Simpson's way. There was unfinished business here. After what had happened to him he would want some sort of retribution, some sort of satisfaction and wouldn't leave until he had it.

And, judging by the trail he was taking, he was heading for Ellis Canyon, not for the Pecons and that caused more suspicions to rear up in Flora McAdam's mind. Was Mr Simpson heading for the Boxed T?

Anxiety clawed at her. He was too sick for that. He should wait for the posse to be formed, as Marshal Patter had insisted, then go with them if he felt he had to. Her advice, if he had asked her for it, would be for him to allow time for the wound he had suffered to heal properly. Indeed, any normal man would be only too glad to do that.

She hurried out of the bedroom and

made for Taw's room. She shook him awake. Taw stared bemused at her as she blurted out what she had seen. Before she had finished, Taw was out of bed.

As he stood erect he said, 'Goddamn it—sorry, Ma—but he ain't no right doin' that.' He began tugging on his pants.

'Fetch him back, Taw,' his mother pleaded while he did, 'explain to him about the posse, Marshal Patter's plan.'

Pulling on his shirt Taw said, 'I'll do my best, Ma. But he's a stubborn man.'

Flora McAdam lifted her chin slightly. 'I have noticed that trait in you, too, son,' she said, almost with a hint of motherly amusement that he should suggest anybody else should have that attribute, but never accepting he had, 'so use it. Maybe you'll prevail.'

Taw grunted, shrugged on his range coat, jerked on his hat. On long legs he strode to the door and pounded down the passageway. Flora McAdam hurried behind him.

As she passed their bedroom door Brad McAdam called, 'Is that you, Ma?'

'It's all right, father,' she called. 'You sleep now.'

Not waiting to find out if she had reassured her husband she hurried on. She found Taw in the tack room. He was already on his way out with his saddle as she reached the door. Taw strode to the corral and selected a mount, a roan he knew had stamina. Soon he had it saddled. He swung up. Flora McAdam put her hand on his leg.

'Be careful, son,' she pleaded. Her face was pale, tight. 'Please.'

Taw's features were set with grim lines. Already, after the traumas of the past two days, the lightness of carefree youth was being eroded from them. The lines of manhood were appearing. He placed his own rough hand on hers. 'Don't fret, Ma, I will,' he said.

Then he headed towards Ellis Canyon, after Carl.

SIXTEEN

His pocket timepiece told Simpson it was 3 a.m. He snapped it shut and stared down the slope at the sprawl of buildings alongside the cottonwood- and alder-lined creek. Two miles back on a wheel-rutted trail he'd come upon he'd found a sign that told him the Boxed T was ahead and there it was.

It seemed quiet. But things being as they were, there must be guards. He couldn't believe Tranter would overlook such a simple precaution. It gratified Simpson to be soon proved right. The glow of a cigarette stabbed the night for a moment, swinging his attention to focus upon it. Near a barn, in the moonlight, he made out the shape of a man.

Fighting the pain still pounding in his

head he began to wonder what he was doing here; began to reckon he was some kind of damned fool to think he could take on the whole of the Boxed T. It had to be a crazy notion.

But here he was.

And that hard fact concentrated his mind. Tranter had used dynamite in Ellis Canyon. That suggested there might be more of that substance still on the ranch, in case the job hadn't been properly done the first time around. If he could get his hands on some sticks of that he could cause all sorts of mayhem down there. He attempted a grin, but winced as pain raged up the side of his face, causing the nausea to seep into him again.

Fighting it, he kept his thoughts working, for insistently, the thing that intrigued him most was: what did Tranter have against him? There had to be more than just the shooting of his gunny, Harkness. But as far as he knew, there was nothing in the past to warrant such persistent deadly attention from the man, such as sending Collins after him when he'd been heading out of this damned basin and out of Tranter's life.

He laid aside the nagging puzzle for the moment. The immediate need was to find that dynamite, if it existed. It could be anywhere. He stared at the ranch-house buildings. There were two huge clapboard barns, a bunkhouse, a small stone building. He stopped his gaze. *Stone* building?

Feeling mildly excited by the discovery he dismounted and tethered his horse in the brush he had paused amongst and moved down the slope. But the first priority, he had to get rid of the guy by the barn.

He moved silently, trying to ignore the hurts that still plagued him, drawing and hefting his Colt as he crept along. It had to be a club. He didn't want noise ... yet.

He reached the back of the barn and worked his way to where he had located the guard's cigarette glow earlier. At the corner he paused, listened, then peered around it. The guard was sitting on a box, staring up the slope that dominated the south side of the house. Presently the guard rose. He began to walk along the barn side, away from Simpson and round the next corner. Simpson cursed silently. Why couldn't the sonofabitch have walked this way and simplified matters?

He padded down the length of the barn, his heart pounding, throbbing more pain into his head. The guard almost bumped into him as he came back around the edge of the building.

Though as startled as the guard, Simpson reacted more swiftly, swung his already poised Colt. It connected with bony noise on the man's skull. The guard grunted then let out a yell, but Simpson's second strike silenced him. However, he had called out momentarily and that could prove serious.

Anxiously, Simpson looked around, saw there was a side door to the barn nearby. Grateful, he holstered his Colt and dragged the man through it and dumped him against the inside wall. He looked as though he might be out for some time.

Simpson went to the door, waited. He half expected a response to the man's yell, but a minute's wait revealed nothing. His tension settling again, Simpson stared at the stone hut once more. That had to be his best bet.

He padded along the barn's clapboard wall again. At the far corner he paused. In the moonlight, the space between the barn and the hut was barren of movement. In fact, there was no sign of activity anywhere.

Uneasy with that, Simpson gazed around him. There *had* to be more guards, but he saw none. Well, to hell with it. Taking a deep breath he loped across to the stone hut. He soon found the door. It was stout. It had a hasp with a padlock through the staple driven into the thick jamb. His gaze searched for something to force it. Then he saw what had to be the smithy, close to the bunkhouse and there had to be something in there he could use. He moved stealthily to it. After a quick search he soon found a steel bar.

He returned to the hut, inserted the bar into the staple and pulled. It came out with a noise similar to a creaking dry hinge. Feeling satisfaction Simpson dropped the bar, pushed the door open. There were tools ... and boxes labelled DYNAMITE. Bullseye! Even better, there were taped rolls of it already prepared, detonated and fused, ready for action. It suggested the job in Ellis Canyon wasn't satisfactorily over yet ...

But hardly able to contain his excitement, Simpson moved to them, took a roll. One would be enough for what he had in mind. He had sulphur matches. All he had to do now was cause some mayhem.

But he didn't have a real plan. He just wanted Tranter, wanted to square accounts. So he had to get the Boxed

T hands occupied, busy at some urgent business, like a dynamited barn blazing in the night. Then, maybe, the chance would come to isolate the Boxed T owner and get out of him what he had against Carl Simpson, ask him why he had sent Collins, then Coke Hewson after him. In his young life Simpson had learnt ways to prise such information from reluctant people. Not polite ways, but ways ...

But the dark shadow closing down the moonshine filtering in through the hut door behind him had him turning, and there was a flurry of noise out there then a gasp. Startling Simpson, the limp form of a man fell into the hut. A Colt was clasped in his hand. The man's head banged against his booted foot. Simpson could see he was out cold.

Staring up swiftly, Simpson saw Taw McAdam's tall shape fill the doorway, Colt in hand, too. He had that damned grin on his face.

'What in the hell are you doin' here?'

Simpson breathed.

Taw said ironically, though clearly a little nonplussed by his harsh reception, 'Well, howdy to you, too.' Then he frowned. 'But you gone clean out of your head, Carl? Comin' here on your own like this? Good job I got to watchin' your back.'

'You trail me?' hissed Simpson.

'How else?' Taw shrugged. 'Ma saw you leave. Woke me. Wants me to persuade you to go back. Some joke, huh? So, what in the hell you aimin' to do?' He grinned again. 'Though I'm with you all the way, I guess.'

Just a dumb kid, thought Simpson. Did he think this was some damned game? But then, he'd been a dumb kid of twenty-one once, facing three vicious gunmen on the streets of Ladderet thinking he was immortal, that death would never touch him—just everybody else in the game of death and it had done ... that time. Yes, Taw was the Carl Simpson of three years ago, he decided. But did he, Carl Simpson, think he was acting any better now after the experience he'd had, to come blundering up here like some damned wet-eared fool once more? Damn it, he was worse than before, for he now knew life wasn't kind and that he wasn't immortal; in fact life, for the most part, was indiscriminate and cruel.

So he nodded. 'OK, Taw,' he growled. 'You're in. That's what you're wantin' me to say, isn't it?'

Taw grinned smugly. 'I figure you ain't much choice,' he said. 'So? You got a plan?'

Simpson glared, irritated that Taw had discovered the tamer of Con Valley was as rash and hotheaded as he was. 'Workin' on it right now. I want Tranter where I can get at him. I want to know what he's got against me. An' I want Hewson. It was that sonofabitch who shot me, wasn't it?'

Taw nodded. 'Yup but tell you later.' He added, 'Dawn'll be here soon, yeah? Can't stand here dickerin' too long.'

'Ain't dickerin',' snorted Simpson. 'Goin' to blow the biggest of the barns. That sit OK with you?'

'Then what?' Clearly doubtful, Taw eyed him, rubbed his square chin. 'Don't sound much of a plan to me.'

Simpson waved a hand impatiently. His damaged head was banging enough, without having Taw McAdam questioning his every damned move. 'Git up on the hillside,' he snorted. 'You got your rifle?'

Taw nodded again. 'Then what agin?'

'Start frightenin' them, if you can.'

'Marshal Patter wants it done right,' pointed out Taw. 'Posse ... the whole works. Ride up, tell them their rights, take them in.'

'He figurin' Tranter will go along with that?' scoffed Simpson. 'Tranter's a curly wolf. A killer. Got to be, the way he gunned down Abel Cross and his boys, if Barras was right. On'y way he's goin' to be dealt with is to be smoked out.'

Taw grinned. 'Been my sentiments

exactly. That son of a coyote forced Pa's hand, had him gunned down. He ain't no friend o' mine, either.'

As a plan was now set in his mind Simpson said, 'So get up on the hillside, Taw. I'll blow one of the barns, then join you. There's bound to be a fire. If it comes to talk, we'll try an' bluff; tell Tranter he's wanted for the murder of Abel Cross and his two hands. Say Harry Barras has spilled the beans in return for clemency. We just don't say he's dead. Tranter won't know unless Hewson's come here an' told him. Then we'll call on him to surrender. He won't know how many of us there is on that hillside.'

Taw shook his head, doubt clearly in his angular features. 'Jesus, he won't cotton to that. You've just said so. It's crazy. Might as well wait for the posse.' His look quickly changed to the quizzical. 'This how you did your lawin' back in Con Valley?'

'Damn it, it worked,' snorted Simpson, 'an' offerin' the chance to them'll make it lawful.' He didn't add some of it had worked in Con Valley with a lot of God's luck, plus the total naïvety of youth and its supposed invincibility. 'So let's git, I'm sick o' damned whisperin'.'

He made for the door and stepped out into the moonlight, almost crazy with the pain in his head. It seemed to be getting worse. Maybe that was what set him out on this stupid stunt. Maybe his brain was so scrambled by the impact of the bullet from that big Sharps it was making him act irrationally.

Then he saw the man coming round the corner of the smaller barn and his gut clamped up. He swayed back into the hut, shoving Taw back with him. But he knew he was too late.

Frantically, he pulled his Colt. There was nothing else for it. He knew he had edged the draw as he saw the guard stagger back, arms wide, his own shot hissing into the sky as Simpson's lead knocked him down. But the thunder of the guns ripped apart the tranquil early morning.

'Git up the bank, Taw,' Simpson rasped urgently. 'The lid's off.'

As Taw ran for the hillside, Simpson pounded for the largest of the barns, fumbling for his sulphur matches along the way. At the big doors he stared in. There were stalls, horses tethered there.

Damn. No way could he kill them.

Shouts were now coming from the bunkhouse, situated on a rise of ground above the creek. Simpson ran to the smaller barn. He saw hay and ranch equipment in there. He struck a match and laid its spluttering flame to the fuse on the roll of dynamite in his hand. It fizzed into life.

With half an eye on the house Simpson tossed the roll on to the hay then ran up the hillside, his head hammering with every stride. The pain of it totally subdued any excitement he might have felt.

He dived into the brush as the mighty roar of the detonation rent the air. He turned to see red-orange flame flare into the dark, planking flying in all directions. Already ignited, fodder flamed upwards. Shouts came from below as Simpson heard Taw call, 'Over here, Carl.'

First Simpson made towards his horse, dragged out his Winchester then joined his friend, who was crouching beside his mount in the bushes.

'We split up,' Simpson ordered immediately, above the noise. 'Case 'em in a crossfire over their heads first off. Let 'em know we're here. We don't kill needlessly.'

Taw nodded and melted into the night.

Simpson stared at the chaos he had caused below. Men were running about shouting. Buckets began to appear. A man was at the hand pump before the ranch-house, drawing water into the trough it fed. A chain was being formed to douse the larger barn that had not been blown, clearly they were giving up on the shattered one already. Two men were already leading the horses out of the larger barn.

Tranter now appeared on the ranch-house stoop and Simpson's gut tightened. Tranter began bawling and pointing. Then Simpson saw Hewson come into view from the brush by the creek. He must have been bedded down back there. Hewson didn't take any notice of the fire. His mean face framed by the lurid flames, he began scanning the hillside above the ranch, then he crouched and moved into the trees. Simpson saw the glint of a knife in his hand.

One real genuine coyote, he thought bitterly.

And seeing Hewson's move, Simpson felt for the deerhorn heft of his own Bowie. He watched as Hewson's shadowy form crept through the moon-silvered night—heading up the slope, heading in his direction. Hewson paused every so often, testing the night like a hunting cougar, head turning, listening.

The dark was now also being illuminated by the flames beginning to flare up from the ruins of the blown barn. Savage, angry flames that reared from the timbers, snapping and crackling their vicious noise. Then Taw's Spencer boomed out from a position a couple of hundred yards west of Simpson.

At the sound of it, swift as a rattler Hewson's head turned, then he dropped from sight. An icy hand tiptoed up Simpson's backbone.

He went into a hunch and padded for Taw's position, picking his route, his feet touching the ground, soft as featherdown. He thought bleakly: Hewson was not the only one who had tracked game ... of all descriptions, except Carl Simpson hadn't done it for money.

Again, in the lurid light, he picked up Hewson's shape. He was snaking through the brush, silent as a diamond back. Taw's Spencer boomed again. The boy was clearly oblivious to Hewson's approach.

Simpson saw now that Hewson could be no more than thirty feet from Taw.

He wanted to call out, warn Taw, but if he did he would lose his own surprise and still maybe not save his friend, maybe even hasten the probability of his death. He picked up his speed. Hewson was concentrated, like a hawk honing in on its prey, not aware that there was another predator closing in on his rear.

Suddenly, Hewson rose, moved forward towards Taw's exposed back, his concentration total. So did Simpson rise, full of singleminded purpose, too. He padded across the ground, breath held, every fibre concentrated on Hewson.

Now Hewson was close enough to lift his blade up for the strike into Taw's undefended back. The young McAdam had his rifle to his shoulder seeking a target below, completely unaware.

Simpson bawled desperately, 'Move, Taw!'

It all happened swiftly after that. Simpson went across the intervening ground, fleet and supple as a cougar closing the final yards to his kill. As he moved he saw Taw was rolling to his right side, swinging round his rifle. Hewson was turning, clearly recognizing he was trapped. His face was a twisted mask of demonic hate in the intense flames of the blazing barn below. He brought his knife up to parry Simpson's thrust. Too late. Simpson felt the spew of Hewson's warm blood on his knife arm, heard his coughing grunt break from him as the blade drove up under Hewson's rib cage and into his heart. He felt Hewson's blade rip through his shirt, missing his lean flank by the width of a panther hair.

'Jesus!' shouted Taw now. His stare was wild, his face taut in the moon and fire glow. He knew he missed death by a split-second. Then he grinned as if seeking something to relieve his fright. 'Well, welcome, partner,' he burbled. 'We-e-e-lcome!'

Simpson found he was shaking. He pushed Hewson's limp body off his blade, the smell of his warm blood sickly sweet in his nostrils. As the body flopped to the ground he said, 'Still got chores to do, Taw. Plan as before.'

'Christ, just like that—after *that?*' Taw breathed. He stared at Hewson's still body.

'Just like that, boy. But it ain't *that* simple.' Simpson raised his hand, showed the tremor in it.

Then he wiped the red-stained blade in the grass, sheathed it, then padded off into the night again to take up his former position. Settling in the brush he pulled the Winchester into his shoulder, fighting to control his shaking limbs. He drew a bead over the heads of the men below. He let off three rapid shots. Then he called, 'Tranter. You're surrounded. The game's up. Barras has split the beans on the Cross killin's.'

He watched the Boxed T owner—who was bawling at his men to stand and fight as they cringed, looking for cover—stop what he was doing and stare at the rim of the hillside.

'Barras is a damned liar,' he bawled after moments. Momentary relief flooded through Simpson. Clearly Tranter didn't know Barras was dead.

Tranter was continuing to scan the hillside defiantly, his face vicious, etched in the angry firelight. Then with hunching movement he made for the cover of the ranch-house doorway, gun out. The men in the bucket chain by now were already dispersed. They were crouching in cover, Colts in hand and peering up the hillside as if awaiting developments.

The barn fire was already threatening to spread to the larger barn. The breeze was wafting the huge flames towards it.

'That bein' the case,' bellowed Simpson taking up the conversation again, 'we can do this all peaceable. Give yourself up an' face trial, Tranter.'

The Boxed T's owner's reply was querulous and harsh. 'Who the hell are you to come up here demandin'? You ain't Patter.'

'It's Carl Simpson, Tranter. Remember me? You seem to have a special interest in me, mister. Beside the other stuff, I want to know why.'

Tranter's reply was wrathful. 'Why, you sonofabitch. Who the hell you think you're bluffin'? I've counted only two guns up there.' He fired off two shots. 'Boys, start earning your damned keep. Get after them up that hill an' smoke them out.'

Taw's Spencer boomed. Lead tore into the jamb above Tranter's head.

'Heed him, Tranter,' Taw called. 'You're on a hidin' to nothin'.'

McAdam's lead forced the Boxed T owner back into the house proper. Tranter mouthed oaths as he went. Then, moments later, he came out again, crouching and firing his Colt. Soon he was into the trees by the creek. As he ran he bawled, 'Damn it, move, boys. Kill those bastards.'

Simpson's glare was fierce. Well, the need required by the law of the land, as he understood it, to give criminals a chance to give themselves up, was fulfilled and he had no qualms now about shooting for real. No more over-the-head shooting. He drew a bead on one of the figures emerging from cover to move up the slope. He fired and saw him stagger back yelling and holding his arm, his Colt dropping from his fingers. He made for the cover of the ranch-house, staring fearfully up the hill. Taw began setting up a steady fire, too. Simpson saw another man drop. But these men didn't appear to be hardcases. Their efforts were too half-hearted.

Then Simpson did a quick scan of the trees below. He couldn't see Tranter. Damn it, he was the sonofabitch he wanted so badly.

SEVENTEEN

Shaking off thoughts of Tranter for now Simpson raked the men below with withering fire. Taw did his share. The blaze of the barn illuminated the scene almost as clear as day and the crossfire they were setting up was clearly concerning the men below.

Then somebody bawled, 'Let's git to the house.'

Simpson counted five hands scuttling across the bare ground. Taw's Spencer downed another one. The man began crawling, trailing a bleeding leg behind him. He finally wriggled into the cover of the ranch-house. Soon gunfire cannoned out from the small windows.

It wasn't exactly what Simpson had had in mind. Then he realized he'd never had anything much in mind, except a need to get back at Tranter, come hell or high water.

He felt the bandages around his head. All the time his skull was pounding. The throbbing continued to nearly drive him crazy. Sometimes he found he had trouble focusing his gaze. It was a crazy state of affairs.

Briefly, he stared east, away from the glare of the fire below. He saw the first pearl-grey hints of dawn paling the sky. He had the feeling this could develop into a long day. But he also felt that a posse would be heading this way before too long, if not already. Taw hadn't returned. Mrs McAdam would be worried sick. She'd have things moving by now for sure, Taw being her only boy.

The boom of a gun from the lip of the draw to his right startled him. The gully was thirty yards away. The draught and heat of lead slashing past his right cheek sent Simpson into a crouch, his anxious gaze sweeping the area. He saw it was Tranter coming over the draw edge, Colt lined up, firing. Simpson stared amazed. Had he gone crazy? More lead burning a path across his neck galvanized him. He fired the Winchester from the hip.

Tranter grunted at the impact of the slug, yet staggered on, firing his Colt and missing until the hammer hit dead shell cases.

From his cover Simpson watched the owner of the Boxed T now stop and stand, while rocking unsteadily on his heels. He seemed to be bemused. Then, with deliberate movements, he started knocking dead brass out of his Colt, ready for reloading.

Simpson stared in disbelief. The crazy ... what was driving Tranter to take such a risk to see him dead?

He ran towards the Boxed T owner. He was clearly wounded bad, but still weakly trying to load his Colt. When he got to him, Simpson beat the weapon out of his hand.

'Now, you sonofabitch,' he rasped harshly. 'Spill it. What's so tasty about my hide?'

Simpson saw, when he raised it to meet his own, Tranter's amber stare was enhanced by the vivid light coming from the fires behind. Then he said bitterly, 'Hewson reckoned he'd done the job on you. Said he thought that Patter an' Taw McAdam were tryin' to bluff him out when they said you were still alive.'

'Still ain't said why you want me so bad, damn it,' snarled Simpson above the roar of guns still hammering away to the rear of him.

A harsh growl broke from Tranter. 'The Mosten boys you killed,' he said. 'Kin o' mine. It's blood for blood, Simpson. That's all. After you kilt 'em I trailed you for a year before I lost you. Then I got sidetracked into other, more profitable things. Damn it, if you hadn't have happened in here, might never have come to anythin', ever.

So damn *you*, mister, fer showin' up. I near had this basin sewn up.'

Tranter gasped, sank to his knees. He pushed aside his corduroy coat and clasped his stomach. Simpson now saw the big patch of blood staining the shirt covering the Boxed T owner's midriff. Then Tranter said, as if in disbelief, 'Jees. Had it made here. Just a few more adjustments an' ... you lousy ...'

Tranter flopped over on to his side, rolled on to his back. Simpson stared into eyes that were gazing back at him, though slowly glazing as death came creeping in. Oddly, Simpson saw there was an ironic twist on Tranter's lips.

Blood for blood? thought Simpson. *Well, mister, you finally got your wish.*

Behind, the crackle of gunfire hotted up and snapped him out of the moment.

He ran back to his position in the brush on the rim of the hill. He could see the large barn had now caught fire. The flames were creeping up the wall that was closest to the dynamited smaller barn. Gun flashes still speared from the small ranch-house windows.

Taw called, 'You OK, Carl? Who was that sonofabitch?'

'Tranter.' Simpson stared down the incline. On a hunch he roared, 'The house. You listenin'? Tranter's dead. You want to go on with this?'

There was silence, a rattle of talk, then the answer came: 'Damn it, mister, we figure we're in too deep to back down now.'

'You'll have a fair trial,' said Simpson. 'I figure Patter to be a straight lawman.'

That prompted further urgent talk. All the time the burgeoning dawn was slowly revealing a still grey range, the higher canyon rimrocks coming up bright orange bulks in the near distance, the tops of the far away Pecons catching the first of the sun.

After a while the spokesman said, fretfully, 'We figure there'll be a lynchin' after those Circle C killin's.'

'Patter won't allow that to happen is my guess,' said Simpson. 'Reckon he'll move you straight to Serela, the county seat, to avoid that.'

'Then what?' demanded the spokesman. 'Hell, most of us here didn't figure Tranter wanted gunsels. An' they're free as birds. Tranter sent them up to the Stoney Ridge line cabin while things developed down here. We hired on to punch cows.'

'You must have guessed there was somethin' fishy,' said Simpson unsympathetically. 'But there'll be a fair trial. Patter'll play it square, right down the line.'

Another man blurted, 'It was Tranter an' Lon Pauler—he's out where Pete said with Freddy Peace and the other hardcases—they killed Cross an' his boys. They're nothin' to do with us, but I guess we were there.'

'That'll be sorted out,' said Simpson. 'While we're jawin' here, how about

Nathan Mather?' drawled Taw. 'Who killed him?'

'Cole Harkness,' shouted a newcomer to the conversation. 'He done it. He's here.'

'You sonofabitch,' another snarled. A gun roared, then another. There were cries. Silence. Simpson stared grimly down at the ranch-house, grey in the still dawn.

After a few moments, the original spokesman said, 'Oh, Goddamn it. This is all goin' to hell here. Harkness's jus' killed Sam Coots fer namin' him. I had to lay Harkness out. He figured all along no way should we be talkin' to you. He's a mean man.'

'I put lead in Harkness,' said Simpson.

'Doc fixed him up,' explained the spokesman. 'Tranter allowed him to rest up in the house.'

'Collins?'

'Died last night.'

'You want to end up like him?' Simpson growled harshly. He was growing impatient. 'We can arrange it.'

More urgent talk rose from the ranch-house. Then, 'You say Bart Tranter's dead?'

'You hear the shootin' just now, near the draw?'

'Yeah.'

'He was on the losin' end.'

There was more heated talk. Finally, somebody bawled, 'We're comin' out, mister. Ain't no pay in dyin'. We'll take our chances with the law.'

Simpson felt relief. He said, 'You've made a wise decision. Throw out your guns, boys, an' follow them, arms raised.'

It was a week later. There'd been a shootout at the Stoney Ridge line cabin. The real hardcases up there had been caught napping. What was left of them when the gunfire died down Patter had handed over to Sheriff Tom Boot in Serela. The cowhands trapped in the ranch-house had talked freely and, it was said, there were pardons on the way.

Marshal Patter stared up at Simpson. 'How's the head?' He was seated behind the small desk in his office, stroking his moustache.

Simpson touched the scar-crusts gingerly. It had been a brutal wound and he'd been fevered for a day or two when the dust had settled at the Boxed T and the adrenalin had stopped pumping. Taw reckoned he'd been fevered while they exchanged lead at the Boxed T! But that was Taw. Doc had taken the bandages off only half an hour ago.

'Pays to be thick-skulled,' he quipped.

'Sheriff Boot said there's a job for you on the county police force,' said Patter seriously. 'He's nearing retirement, so there could be promotion in it.'

Simpson pursed his lips while probing the still-massive brown-blue bruising down the side of his face. Then he said, 'John, I've pushed my methods of bein' a lawman to the limits. There's got to come a day when the luck runs out.'

Patter gave out with one of his rare grins. 'Reckon Tom Boot'll steady you down.'

'Maybe,' said Simpson. 'But I ain't takin' the chance. Still headin' for California.'

Standing near the office window, Taw grinned at him. He had his arm around Lucy Cross. They'd come into town an hour ago to see the preacher about arranging the wedding, and to say goodbye to Carl.

'You've got a one track mind,' he said, 'keep goin' on about California. That notion's got you into all sorts of trouble recently.'

Simpson returned the smile. 'Won't this time, partner, 'less some sonofabitch takes my hoss agin.'

At that, Taw roared with laughter. When he'd finished he said, 'Well, at least stay for the weddin', damn it.'

Simpson considered that proposition for the umpteenth time, then shook his head once more. 'Not a chance. Might finally git talked into stayin' on. You got a silk tongue sometimes, Taw.'

'You just tumbled that's why I keep askin'?' Taw stared, as if surprised.

Still full of good humour they all moved out into the sunlit main street of Hell. Simpson climbed easily into the saddle and grinned down. 'Taw, you once bid me *Welcome to Hell.* Well, I guess it's a fond goodbye, this time.' He stared at them, ranked on the boardwalk. 'Been good knowin' you all. *Adios, amigos.* '

He raised a hand and wheeled his mount and headed off up the street towards the Pecons. Somehow, he figured his journey wouldn't be interrupted this time. And further, he had the feeling that the next time he came this way there really would be a Welcome to Hell.

This Large Print Book for the Partially sighted, who cannot read normal print, is published under the auspices of

THE ULVERSCROFT FOUNDATION